About the author

Gilly was born in Blackpool, England. She lived for several years in Germany, and later in Canada. Gilly taught English and drama for some years, then developed a practice as a workshop facilitator. She lives in Derbyshire.

ALBA AND THE LADY OF THE FLOWERS

GILLY WILMOT

ALBA AND THE LADY OF THE FLOWERS

Vanguard Press

A CIP catalogue record for this title is
available from the British Library.

ISBN 978 1 80016 394 2

Vanguard Press is an imprint of
Pegasus Elliot MacKenzie Publishers Ltd.
www.pegasuspublishers.com

First Published in 2022

Vanguard Press
Sheraton House Castle Park
Cambridge England

Printed & Bound in Great Britain

Chapter 1
A Sad Time for Alba

Alba sat quietly, listening to her grandmother's laboured breathing. She knew Nooka was dying because her mother had explained carefully what would change in Nooka's breathing as her life began to finally ebb away. Alba knew that this day would come, but in her heart, she wished that somehow a miracle would happen and that her beloved Nooka would just be as she had been all Alba's life. She closed her eyes and concentrated on a picture of Nooka and herself together in the garden. From being a toddler, Nooka had made the garden magical for Alba in so many ways. Nooka had taught the little girl the names of flowers and trees, often weaving in a story.

Alba smiled, remembering herself at about three years old. The lady next door was expecting a baby and told Alba that babies came from daffodils. Alba told Nooka that the lady did not know that fairies live in daffodils and, anyway, babies come from mummies' tummies. Alba laid her head on Nooka's bed near to the old lady's hand which twitched fitfully. Still thinking about fairies, she dozed off.

**

Nooka's thoughts were wandering. She was gathering watercress for her mother. The reserve where the small family lived had many streams meandering through the nearby forest. The sun was hot on her skin. Strands of her long dark hair stuck to her face as she reached for the best bunches of cress. Her mother would be pleased with her. Nooka sat back frowning. In a few days, she would have to attend the school run by the Department of Indian Affairs. All tribal children between seven and fifteen had to go. Some attended the day school. Others were forced to leave home and live in, like it or not. Nooka's father had pleaded with the Department of Indian Affairs for his thirteen—year-old daughter to be allowed to remain on the reserve, only to be refused. This was the situation throughout Canada. The only consolation for Nooka's parents was that their daughter would attend the day school and not be sent away to a residential facility. Nooka had heard her parents whisper quietly together in worried voices. Fragments of that conversation stayed in her mind. 'Forced to speak English'. 'Beat the Indian out of them'.

***

Alba awoke suddenly, aware of her grandmother's hand pressing upon her head.

'What is it, Nooka? Are you in pain? Shall I get Mum?' Alba sat up sharply.

Nooka's mouth was working but no sound came out. Her breathing was still laboured. Every now and then, she muttered words that Alba could barely hear and were not in English. Should she run and fetch her mother? Confused, she reached out to hold the old lady's hand, squeezing gently. 'I'm here, dear Nooka, Alba's here.' She fancied her grandmother had become calmer and her breathing not quite so laborious. Her limbs relaxed.

***

Nooka was remembering a walk in her favourite part of the forest, free from her hated school for the day. She gave a little skip, laughing at the antics of a nearby chipmunk which chirruped as it ran up-and-down over a tree stump. Nooka gazed into the animal's dark little eyes, feeling envious of this tiny creature's freedom. There were rustling sounds in the undergrowth. Nooka tensed. Bears were common in this part of the forest. Mostly they were black bears, so not so scary as the grizzlies, but one had to be careful. Nooka knew to not ever approach the cute little black bear cubs, tempting as it was. Mother bear would not hesitate to attack if a human came near her cubs.

'Hello there.' A young man stood a few yards away, smiling. 'Lovely morning, miss.'

Nooka gazed up at him, shyly sweeping her long black braids over her shoulders, prepared to make a dash for it if necessary. She was a good runner and could outrun him, she felt sure. Studying him, she saw a medium-height young white man. His hair was jet black and curly, framing a sensitive face. He blinked large brown eyes.

'*Bonjour, mademoiselle, je suis* Pierre.'

Nooka stared intently. She had heard her father speak of the French loggers who were in the area, and he had warned her to keep her distance. Brown eyes twinkled and a broad smile revealed even white teeth. Nooka could feel herself blushing under his gaze. Around them, the sounds of the forest continued and yet it seemed they were in a world apart, each searching the other with wide dark eyes. Looking, searching, finding. And that is how it began; Nooka's first and only love—the father of her beloved daughter.

***

Alba shifted position. Her back was stiff. She realised that it had grown dark in the little bedroom. The old lady's face was relaxed. The corners of her mouth lifted in a slight smile. Alba reached over to switch on the bedside lamp but checked herself. Was she imagining it or did the room seem to be getting lighter just around her grandmother's bed? The house was quiet. There were no lights on in the nearby landing or outside in the garden and yet Alba was aware of a gentle steady light surrounding Nooka. She reached out to touch Nooka's cheek, soft and warm as always. So many years of nestling up to her beloved Nooka, feeling safe and comforted. Perhaps, she should go to fetch her mother now. This light in the room was puzzling yet comforting at the same time. Yes, her mother could come and sit with her now.

A few minutes, five at the most, and Alba and her mother entered the bedroom quietly. Alba stood back as her mother approached the bedside. Still the room had a trace of that special light Alba had experienced. Camille bent to kiss her mother's forehead and as she rose, Alba saw the tears glistening in her mother's dark eyes. 'She's gone, Alba.'

***

The next few days were especially difficult for Alba. She went to school as usual even though her parents said it would be all right for her to miss a few days. Somehow, the routine of getting up at the usual time, putting on her school uniform, sorting out her schoolbag, helped her to feel that she had a sort of control of her life. In a funny kind of way, she felt that if she made life normal, then maybe Nooka would return and life would resume the pattern she had got used to. Of course, at twelve, she knew old people died, it was not unusual. Her best friend Molly had been through the experience of losing her grandfather last year. Molly, however, did not seem to be much affected, perhaps because she did not see very much of him. He lived a long way from Molly and her parents seldom mentioned him. When the news came that granddad had passed away, Molly received the news rather matter-of-factly, as though it was a stranger and not her parent's parent. Alba remembered Molly telling her about her mother's reaction to her grandfather's death.

'Well then, that's that. We were never close, anyway.'

At the time, Alba did not pay much attention. It just never crossed her mind that anything would ever happen to Nooka. She had always been a huge presence throughout Alba's life. It was inconceivable that that would change.

At breakfast, her parents were discussing what was to take place in the next few days. Nooka had already been taken away to the funeral home. They came early that morning. Alba stood in the doorway of her bedroom as two men dressed in black spoke in hushed tones to her mother.

'Darling, go back to bed. Dad and I will deal with this. It's better that you stay in your room for the moment.'

Eventually, Alba heard the front door close and the sound of a vehicle being driven away. She crossed over the landing to Nooka's bedroom. Everything was the same but not the same. The clothes, furniture, little ornaments, Nooka's bits and bobs were all in their usual places. A beam of sunlight was catching something on the floor by Nooka's bed; her glasses, her newish half-moon glasses.

'Do you think I'll see the moon better?' chuckled Nooka when they had got back from the optician.

Alba lay on the bed pulling the old eiderdown over her head. Nooka didn't like duvets. She insisted on keeping an extremely old and faded eiderdown. 'I've always slept so well for years under it so why change now?'

Alba sobbed, her tears wetting Nooka's pillow which had traces of her favourite floral perfume. Her grandmother loved all flowers, teaching Alba from an early age the names of the many flowers in their garden. Nooka knew how to gather lavender and put bunches in to cotton bags. 'A lavender bag under your pillow smells nice and helps you to sleep well, Alba,' she had said, smiling warmly.

Her parents stood from the breakfast table, concerned eyes, a loving hug from each. 'You know you don't have to go to school today,' her father said quietly. 'Mum's not going in for a few days. She has compassionate leave.'

Alba's mother taught English and French at the local college. This worked well for the family. As a senior social worker, Alba's father often had to work irregular hours, so Alba was able to have a lift to and from school with her mother.

***

'What was Tom doing in the garden?' Miss Jenkins asked the class.

A few hands went up. Alba's gaze was concentrated on a blackbird outside the window struggling to prise a worm from the grass.

Lucy Jenkins regarded Alba thoughtfully. The girl loved stories and usually paid rapt attention when "*Tom's Midnight Garden*" was being read. Lucy knew Alba's mother quite well and was aware of the family's bereavement. She sighed and continued reading. Alba was one of her brightest pupils, thoughtful and creative. She was what could be described as dreamy, inclined to oversensitivity, finding some aspects of school life hard to deal with. Her schoolmates could be thoughtlessly unkind. Alluding to her darker skin and long black hair was one example. Fortunately, Alba's best friend Molly was a blessing in this case. Good-humoured and outgoing, Molly's easy-going, affectionate nature made her a very popular girl. Slightly stocky, she had curly blonde hair in a ponytail and bright blue eyes. She staunchly stuck by her friend and rebuked her classmates in no uncertain terms if they hurt her. Molly's general popularity meant that she could be quite challenging when defending Alba and most of the children accepted this.

At break time, Miss Jenkins asked Alba to stay behind. 'I'm so sorry about your grandmother,' she said gently. 'This must be such a sad time for you. I remember meeting your Nooka — that was her name, wasn't it? — several times. She was a lovely lady.'

Alba studied a little spider creeping along the top of the desk. 'Yes, miss.'

'I'm always here to talk, Alba, if you would like someone to talk to, that is. I know that words are pretty inadequate on these sorts of occasions,' she added.

Alba looked at her teacher, finding it difficult to respond. Miss Jenkins was her favourite teacher and she knew she was being genuinely kind. She turned away, aware that her eyes were beginning to prick with tears.'

'I need to go now, miss,' she murmured through a tight throat.

Somehow, the school day seemed interminably long. Alba found it difficult to concentrate in any of the lessons and longed for the time when her mother would come to fetch her home. Finally, she was putting everything in her school bag.

'Would you like to come round to mine later?' asked Molly. 'I could introduce you to my new rabbit, Ollie. He's so sweet and you could cuddle him.'

Alba smiled faintly. 'I would like to see Ollie, but I think I should be at home at the moment. Mum and Dad are making arrangements for Nooka's funeral and I want to know what is going to happen.'

Molly looked thoughtful. She knew how deeply her friend felt things. Alba worried a lot. She got upset about stuff that did not really affect Molly so much. One day, out playing, they came across a dead baby rabbit that they learned later had died from myxomatosis. Alba was inconsolable. How could such a nasty disease kill that innocent little creature? Molly was upset, of course, but not to the same extent as Alba. Yes, playing with little Ollie would be a good thing.

Molly had plans. She had received a second-hand laptop for her birthday. There were so many exciting things she could look at on her new toy. Well, it wasn't really a toy. Her parents had told her to be very careful with it. A cousin of Molly's who was thirteen had told her about chat rooms. This sounded exciting and Molly loved exciting things. She would go home and look up chat rooms.

The day of Nooka's funeral arrived. Alba's father David looked very smart in his dark suit, with his hair newly trimmed. Alba loved her father. A quiet, thoughtful man, he took his social work career very seriously, caring for each and every one of his clients. Sometimes, he would come home late, exhausted, with a haunted look in his eyes. When Alba was old enough, he explained how some cases, particularly those involving children, were distressing. When she was little, she would clamber up onto his lap and put her arms around his neck.

'Don't be sad, Daddy. Look, I've drawn a picture for you.'

As she grew older, she became aware that her father needed to spend time quietly in his study listening to music if he had had a demanding day. However, he always made time to listen to his daughter however tired he was.

Alba watched her mother carefully brush her long dark hair, arranging it into a stylish chignon. Like Alba, she had luminous brown eyes, which she turned to peruse Alba in the mirror. Smiling wistfully, Camille sighed. 'I miss her so much, Alba. I can't believe it has all happened so quickly. One minute she was fine and then, she seemed to fade so fast. Still, she didn't suffer. For that I'm so grateful. She went peacefully, I think.'

Alba took her mother's hand gently. She knew how much her grandmother had meant to Camille. Over the years, she had told Alba about Nooka's life in Canada.

***

West Coast of Canada, 1968

Nooka Ducharme sat by her favourite stream. Usually, it was where she picked watercress for her mother. Today, there weren't any. She sighed and half-heartedly ran her fingers through the water. As always, it was perfectly clear. Small coloured stones glinted in the sun. Nooka's mother used to tell her that the water spirits painted the stones and arranged them in patterns that they liked. At six years old, Nooka had loved this story. Each time she came to the stream, she gazed intently to see if the stones were in different places.

Nooka sighed again. She was tired and her back hurt. All the previous day, she had been made to sit bolt upright at her desk in school. Not allowed to turn round, or go the facilities to relieve herself. Nooka forced herself to concentrate her gaze straight ahead. The master of the class looked at her coldly with small deep-set eyes, defying her to fidget. That would mean the following day she would have to suffer the same treatment. Small droplets of sweat began to dot her brow. No. She would not wet herself. She would not give the master the satisfaction of further humiliation.

Her crime had been committed hours earlier during the morning prayer—in English, of course. All day every day, the master spoke only English to the children. Nothing else was permitted. If a child spoke in their native language, punishment was immediate and severe. A caning, usually on the hand, but sometimes it would turn into a savage beating. One or two of the masters took a sadistic pleasure from injuring their young charges for the smallest of perceived misdemeanours.

Nooka had been silently mouthing the words of an old tribal song during the morning prayer. Though her lips were scarcely moving, the prayer master happened to briefly glance at her. That was enough. The 'chipmunk', as Nooka called him because of his deep-set sharp little eyes, stood still. He gazed at Nooka with a look of cold contempt.

'Sit, girl.' The other children shifted nervously. Someone hiccupped. 'Be silent, all of you!' Chipmunk was beside Nooka in two strides, his hands pressing hard on her shoulders, forcing her back to straighten painfully against the rough wooden chair. 'You will sit without moving for the entire day, you hear me? Not one movement or it's the birch for you. I know what you were doing and if you ever attempt that again, I'll beat the Indian out of you.'

The entire class quailed at those words, so often repeated by the masters. They were told to forget their own language and speak only English. The cry 'We'll beat the Indian out of you' haunted everyone in the school.

***

'Camille, Alba, the car is here.' Alba's father stood in the hallway waiting as his wife and daughter came down the stairs and into the car.

Alba sat between her parents in the small chapel. An old friend of Nooka had arranged the flowers. Years before, Nooka had taught Mrs Bunning how to arrange flowers. Nooka was often invited to the Women's Institute to give talks about her early life. She took some persuading at first, because Nooka did not speak readily to strangers about her past. She was also anxious about her heritage and if people would accept her.

She had moved from Canada to England when Camille and David married and had lived with the family thereafter until her death. The ladies of the Women's Institute took Nooka to their hearts from the beginning. Her gentle nature, knowledge of flowers and herbs and love of people they found very appealing. The ladies also received valuable insights from Nooka about tribal life and, more importantly, about the tragedy of the residential schools.

Hymns were sung. Alba's parents and various other people spoke of her grandmother, her effect on those whose lives had been touched by this remarkable woman. Tears rolled down Alba's cheeks but she did not wipe them away. Instead, she remembered Nooka walking in the garden, touching some of the large stones near the rockery. Nooka had paused, placing her hand gently on a beautiful large grey stone in the corner. She often sat there on warm days soaking up the sun, lost in thought.

'Do you know, Alba, about some of my friends who managed to survive being sent away to the residential schools? They told me they had to learn to suppress natural feelings of love, compassion and gentleness. They became so lost and lonely, they developed hearts of stone to cope.'

Alba was shocked. 'But Nooka, weren't they allowed to see their parents for holidays?'

Nooka smiled sadly. Quietly, she explained that many children were completely separated from their community for many years. 'They came to believe their parents no longer loved them.' She reached out to Alba. 'Darling child, always be loving and kind, especially to yourself. Never let your heart turn to stone, no matter what happens in your life.'

Later that evening, Alba's parents sat quietly talking downstairs. Alba gazed around her bedroom. She really ought to sort out her collection of bears which held pride of place on most of her shelves. She was particularly fond of her black bear and little cubs. They were a constant reminder of Canada and Nooka. Maybe she should tidy away some of her other cuddly toys. After all, she was not a little girl any more. After today, she was feeling different, more grown up. Life would not be the same any more, she knew. She drew the curtains and switched on the small bedside light. Turning down the brightly coloured quilt her grandmother had made, she lay down. The phone rang, making Alba jump.

'Alba, it's me, Molly.' Her friend's voice sounded excited. Molly often became excited about things. Alba liked that because she herself was not inclined that way. *'Maybe I'm a bit dull,'* she thought.

'What is it? I've been to Nooka's funeral and I'm a bit tired, Molly.'

'You won't believe it. I've really got the hang of these chat rooms. You know, the stuff you can do on your computer. And,' Molly paused dramatically, 'I have made a friend. He's a bit older than me—fourteen. He's going to send me a picture.'

Alba sighed. 'Um… OK,' she replied. Feeling quite tired now, she decided to call Molly the following morning.

Chapter 2
The Voice in the Garden

Miss Jenkins was concerned. Several weeks had passed since Alba's grandmother died, but she was still withdrawn. This seemed to Lucy Jenkins more than Alba's frequent dreamy moods. Was she depressed, she wondered? She knew that it was not uncommon for children to exhibit symptoms of depression. Sadly, she reflected on the concerns of some of her colleagues, especially the older ones. They would frequently mention that in the many years they had spent in the teaching profession, cases of depression in children had increased rather a lot in recent years. Lucy Jenkins frowned, her usually smooth features looking troubled. Parents' evening was coming up soon. She planned to speak to Camille and David Anderson. It was important to ask how Alba was doing at home, her moods and so forth.

***

Alba jumped as a small ball of crumpled paper hit her ear. She turned round impatiently. Why did

Molly need to attract her attention that way? Why couldn't she just tap her arm or something? She sighed. Molly was her best friend. After all, she did not have many friends. Ignoring Molly would not be a good idea. Miss Jenkins was writing something on the board, her back turned from the class.

'What is it?' Alba whispered.

Molly grinned, her blonde curls bouncing around as usual. Blue eyes sparkling with Molly mischief. 'I've got a picture now. You know, that boy I met on the chat room? He's gorgeous. He thinks I'm thirteen.' Molly giggled.

'Get on with your work, Molly!' said Miss Jenkins sharply. Molly reddened but she quickly took up her pen and continued to complete the comprehension exercise. Molly liked Miss Jenkins. Her lessons were interesting and she was always fair. She never made any of the class feel humiliated if they got things wrong. *Not like some of the teachers,* Molly thought with a grimace. Mr Evans their maths teacher, for example. He really seemed to enjoy it when someone made a mistake. He also encouraged others in the class to join in the laugh. Molly hated this. It went against the grain for her to see a classmate made a fool of, boy or girl.

Milling around in the playground, children gathered together in various noisy little groups. It was morning break, and many were sharing sweets and other small snacks. Molly drew her friend over to the large tree which overhung one corner of the yard.

'Look at this, Alba.' Molly surreptitiously drew her mobile phone from her pocket.

Alba gasped. 'Molly, we're not supposed to keep our phones all the time. How come you didn't put yours in the box this morning?'

Molly shrugged. 'Mrs Bennet was chatting to Mr Wilson so I sneaked past and she didn't see me.'

Alba sighed. 'Oh, come on then, let's have a look.'

Molly's fingers flew over her phone pressing one button with a flourish. 'There, isn't he gorgeous?'

Alba peered over her friend's shoulder. The smiling face of a boy with floppy brown hair and nice even features could be clearly seen on the screen. 'Oh,' said Alba. 'He does look nice. How old is he? What's his name?'

Molly drew herself up proudly. 'His name is Tim. He's fourteen and ever so clever. He sends me lots of texts.' She laughed. 'He even loves all the same songs as me. We chat all the time. That's why I keep my phone with me. I get so many texts from him.'

Alba frowned. She knew her friend was impulsive and really friendly but something about what Molly was doing made her anxious. She did not really know why she felt this. After all, Tim seemed really nice and her friend was very happy. Alba's parents limited her use of computer and phone, especially the latter. She mostly used her computer for her schoolwork. She did not take much interest in the games other people played on theirs.

Sometimes, she would look up information about wildlife in other parts of the world. Alba loved animals. One day, she hoped to visit a baby elephant sanctuary she had heard about. It was in Africa, a continent she was also hoping to visit. So many wonderful wild animals to see. One of the boys in her class came from Botswana. In one of Miss Jenkin's lessons, the class were encouraged to stand up and say a few words about the things they would like to know more about in the world. Alba was fascinated to hear about Botswana and resolved there and then that this would be a place she would definitely visit.

Finally, three thirty came and Alba was making her way out of the classroom.

'I've just finished marking your comprehension exercise, Alba, it was excellent,' said Miss Jenkins.

'Thank you, miss,' muttered Alba, quickening her step.

'I meant what I said the other day, Alba. If at any time you feel it might help to talk about how you feel at the moment, I...' Lucy Jenkins hesitated. Taking a deep breath, she began, 'Alba, I lost someone too when I was just a bit older than you.' Lucy bit her lip. Was it OK for her to share this with Alba? At twelve, Alba was very mature for her years but she was clearly suffering.

Lucy made up her mind. If sharing her experience with Alba might help her, she would continue. 'My mother died when I was thirteen. She had been poorly for a long time. I can remember how tired and out of breath she became just walking down the street where we lived. I helped her as much as I could with housework and cooking, but she got weaker and weaker.'

Alba looked into the kind face of her teacher. She put her schoolbag on the back of a chair, sat and listened.

'My father was wonderful, Alba. He never said a word when his shirts weren't ironed, meals not ready or the bathroom got really dirty. He just smiled and held my mother in his arms. He knew how frustrated she got in those final years and months, not being able to manage the house; a point of pride for her. It was awful to see her weeping quietly while struggling to make the beds or do a bit of cleaning.'

Alba nodded thoughtfully. 'It must have been really hard for you and your dad. Nooka wasn't ill for a long time, and Mum said she did not suffer before she died. So, I know I should be grateful for that.'

'Dear Alba, there is no "should be" in these situations,' Lucy said gently. 'I'm really sharing this with you because I know how awfully painful it is to lose someone that you love very much. We all have to deal with it as best we can. So, the word "should" is not appropriate here. We try to find our own way to grieve. There is no right way or wrong way. At thirteen years old, I really struggled losing my mother so soon. I thought she would be with me always.'

Alba smiled sadly. 'I thought that about Nooka. I could never imagine a time in my life when she would not be there.' Alba suddenly seemed to shrink in the chair. Her shoulders shook as she began to weep. Head in hands, she cried so hard her tears pooled on the table in front of her. Lucy Jenkins remained still and quiet. She knew not to reach out to Alba yet but to let the girl cry freely, let the tears flow. She knew that this weeping was an important part of healing. Oh, how she had wept herself, all those years ago. She still wept sometimes when she thought about her mother.

Alba's sobbing gradually began to ease. She turned her tearstained face towards her teacher. 'Will this ever get better, miss? I feel so awful.'

Lucy laid her hand gently on Alba's shoulder. 'Yes, it will, it will. Be assured of this. But you know it really is a matter of time. Time does heal. I know that will sound difficult to believe now, but eventually, the pain of grief will be less. One day, you will find you can think about Nooka and it will not hurt so much.'

***

The snow crunched under her boots as Nooka walked briskly to her favourite spot. The forest seemed still and hushed under a deep layer of snow. The sound of the stream trickling seemed loud in contrast. Nooka wrapped her furs around her tightly, hands deep in large warm mittens. She had spent nearly a year attending the school and was finally able to face the time there with less dread. Finding ways to cope with the unrelentingly harsh days spent there had become somewhat easier.

Although she feared the masters and was on her guard constantly, in case she displeased any of them, she was adjusting. Of course, coming home each day kept her going physically, mentally and emotionally. For that, she was very grateful. Her parents listened patiently to her description of life at the school. She was, however, careful to censor out the worst parts. Her parents were worried enough about her without burdening them further.

She shivered despite her warm furs, remembering a particular lesson a few days ago. Almost every day, the masters took every opportunity to turn the children away from their parents and tribal ways. On this occasion, the master told the class, 'You can't live like your parents any more. You are dirty and they don't have anything. They are poor.' The class were told they were good-for-nothing Indians and they would not go far in life.

Nooka had listened to all this with her heart in her mouth. Suddenly, it was forbidden to have any good memories of themselves. The native teachings, the drum ceremonies, indeed anything of her native culture was condemned and, worst of all, to be forgotten forever. Nooka found it hard not to blurt all this out at home. How could she? Her parents would be devastated. No, somehow, she had managed to steel herself against mentioning all that.

Being outside in nature helped her to cope. She walked every day if she could, bathed in the dappled light between the giant forest trees, the illuminated dust motes dancing around her. Nooka imagined these little dots of light to be nature spirits or tree sprites. Her painful time at the school receded a little during her forest walks. She imagined washing the horrid school experience away as she bathed her hands in the stream watching these bad things float away. But most of the time, she carried a deep pain in her heart. The pain of loss was increasing as her time in the school went on. She thought of it as a prison of despair. Each day, she was being forced to separate herself in her mind from those she loved and a life that she loved. Nooka knelt by the stream, banked by the pure white snow. Slowly, tears fell, their warmth melting tiny patterns in the snow.

***

Molly sat curled up on her bed. She had just received a really exciting text from Tim. Earlier that day, when she got home from school, she sent him a text. She took several photos of herself before deciding on one that she thought would do. Her mother's makeup bag had been really useful. Molly felt a bit guilty about that. Still, she had only used a little mascara and eyeliner. Her blue eyes were her best feature, she thought as she smiled into her phone. Blonde curls had been swept back from her face. Satisfied, Molly judged she could pass for thirteen and sent the picture to Tim.

Almost immediately, her phone pinged. It was Tim. He thought she looked fantastic and could not wait to meet her. In fact, he wondered how soon she could come to a special place he had in mind. '

That was quick,' Molly thought. *'He must really be keen. It's getting late, but I must call Alba and tell her the latest'.*

***

Alba slept well that night. She went over her conversation with Miss Jenkins earlier that day. It really seemed to help, especially when Miss Jenkins told her in such detail about the loss of her own mother. Alba felt a small twinge of embarrassment. *'Oh dear, I really did blub, didn't I? Still, Miss Jenkins won't say anything,'* she thought.

Alba woke to find the sun streaming in through the window, making her face quite hot. It was Saturday so no school, thank goodness. Not that she disliked school. Quite the opposite. in fact. She loved English and drama—particularly drama. Hopefully, now that she had moved to secondary school there would be more plays. Acting was something Alba loved. At junior school, her hand always shot up when the chance came to play a role. Her starring role as Alice in *'Alice in Wonderland'* had won high praise all round. One day, Alba would go to drama school and become a real actress. This would be her dream job, she thought.

The garden was beginning to bloom with all the spring flowers that Alba's grandmother could fit into the medium-sized garden.

'Look, Alba!' Nooka had cried one spring day. 'The sun has painted the garden yellow.'

On her way outside, Alba passed the open door of the kitchen, pausing as she heard her mother's raised voice.

'This job is really getting you down, David. Surely there's something else you could do? You're so moody these days. Can't you...?'

'For goodness' sake, Camille! No, I can't do something else. This is my job and I'm not just walking away. Oh, I haven't got time for this. I'm going to my study.'"

Alba stood by the back door. She loved her parents deeply and hated seeing them upset. On impulse, she went to her father's study and knocked quietly on the door.

'Dad?' she called tentatively.

In his study, her father sat slumped in his chair.

'Go away, Alba, I'm busy!' growled David.

Over the past few months, he had been dealing with a particularly distressing case. The family concerned were struggling on many fronts; a disabled mother and an unemployed father who drank heavily most of the time. Their three children aged three to twelve were deemed at risk. Sadly, when their father had a drunken episode, he hit his wife and children. The twelve-year-old girl had tried her best to protect and look after her mother and two younger siblings. Not surprisingly, she was struggling to keep up at school.

Matters had really come to a head when the mother was admitted to hospital with severe bruising and some cracked ribs. David had no option. He had to recommend that the children be taken away from home. A place of safety was vital now for the children, who desperately wanted to stay together. So far, this was proving difficult. David had not yet found a foster home that was willing to take all three children.

Alba slipped quietly into the garden. She sighed deeply, thinking that sometimes life seemed more difficult as she got older. When she looked towards the far end of the garden, the thought came to her that she was leaving some of her childhood behind. She sensed that she was already starting to think, see and behave differently. Immediately, she wished Nooka was there now. Her grandmother was always ready to listen to Alba. Worries were always smaller after Alba had confided in Nooka and her world a safer place.

A bright shaft of sunlight illuminated the large grey stone at the bottom of the garden. This was where her grandmother came to sit most days even in snowy weather. Nooka would perch herself on the stone, wrapped up warmly, smiling at Alba.

'Come and sit beside me, child. Listen to the sounds, see the beauty that surrounds us here.'

Alba wandered slowly down the old flagged garden path. The daffodils were in full bloom, their sweet scent reaching Alba as she breathed in the morning air.

Conveniently, the old stone had the kind of shape that made it a comfortable seat. It had been there when her parents bought the house. The previous owners said it was very old. But they had no idea how it had come to be in the garden. It was very large and not easy to move, something of a mystery. Alba wondered how long it had stood there and how it came to be in an ordinary suburban garden. It had some strange markings on it and she was curious about what they meant. However, her parents said they thought the markings were just the result of the stone being weathered over the years. Nonetheless, as an imaginative child, Alba liked to think that the mysterious markings had a meaning. Maybe, it was an ancient stone inscribed with something important, a mystery she could solve one day.

Alba arranged herself in a comfortable position. The warm spring sun shone on her long dark hair. Fortunately, her darker skin seemed to tolerate sunshine quite well. Alba grimaced, remembering an incident a few months ago. She was on her way to a maths lesson, the corridor full of children's noisy chatter. She was preoccupied with her forthcoming role in '*Lost at Sea*'. Miss Jenkins had chosen her to play Harriet in the end of year play. Harriet was the leading role. Alba was so excited by this; she was learning her words quickly and practicing her moves in front of her bedroom mirror. Nearing the door to Mr Benson's classroom, she had heard girlish giggles.

'She doesn't look like Harriet. She's too dark. Harriet has fair hair and is pale.'

Alba winced at the memory. Several girls and boys in her year had parents or grandparents from other parts of the world. Alba had never been concerned about the colour of people's skin but she knew that some children were.

A blackbird was singing loudly in the cherry tree, a robin hopped about near Alba's feet. She found herself relaxing, letting some worrisome thoughts go. There was no wind, the air seemed almost to still around her. Alba felt a bit sleepy in the warm sun. Her eyelids drooped. She really did feel better now.

Alba closed her eyes. She had the impression that the scent of the daffodils had become stronger in the last few minutes. Although the birds were still singing and the leaves rustled gently, Alba felt aware of a deep silence and what felt like another person standing near her.

'Alba,' came a faint whisper. Alba opened her eyes quickly; thinking perhaps her mother had come out to see her. There was no one there.

'*I must have imagined it,*' thought Alba, '*or maybe I just drifted off.*' She shrugged and closed her eyes again.

'Alba.' The whisper came louder this time.

Startled, Alba looked around her carefully. Again, no one there. A slight breeze lifted her hair gently then all became still again.

'Don't be afraid,' the voice clearly said. 'I love the garden too. The flowers are beautiful.'

Curiously, Alba remained quite relaxed. This was all a bit strange but not scary at all. In fact, the voice had a comfortable feel; gentle like the breeze that had wafted her hair moments ago.

'Are you... what, erm...?' Alba stumbled, quite unsure of the right thing to say under the circumstances.

'About the flowers,' the voice continued. 'What do you see when you look at them?' Alba touched her stone seat with both hands. Yes, reassuringly, it was still there. Was she dreaming? Maybe she had dozed off. Feeling confused, Alba stood up, took a few paces forward, then back to the stone. The voice came again in the same, even, gentle tone. 'What do you see, Alba?'

A large clump of daffodils grew very near to the stone seat. Alba decided to concentrate her gaze on them. Staring until her eyes began to water, she said hesitantly, 'Well, I see very pretty daffodils which are quite tall and very yellow. They also smell lovely. Oh, and they have sort of trumpet-shaped petals in the middle of them,' she said.

'Good,' came the reply. Alba felt herself relaxing a little. 'Now, Alba, I want you to close your eyes and try to picture the daffodil in your mind. Can you do that?"'

'Yes,' Alba replied quietly.' I love trying to imagine things.' She settled, became still, eyes closed.

'Can you see the daffodils?'

'Yes.'

'Now try to remember the smell of the flowers.'

Alba concentrated. She found it easy to picture the daffodil but recalling its scent was harder. She bit her lip. 'This is more difficult. I can see the flower easily but not smell it.'

There was a soft laugh. 'Ah, yes. You see, Alba, you have several senses; sight, hearing, touch, smell and taste. These are your physical senses; the way you connect to the physical world.'

'Mmm,' said Alba. 'You mean I use these all the time?'

'Yes. Now ask yourself which of these senses are you most aware of, do you think?'

Alba thought carefully. 'All of them, I think. Pretty equally.'

The voice continued gently, 'Think harder, Alba. Do you use each sense equally all the time or are there one or more senses that you use more often?'

Concentrating deeply now, Alba fell silent for several minutes. Of course, she always used her eyes and ears. Likewise, she liked to touch things. She loved to caress the soft, furry cat next door. Alba was like her mother and grandmother who were very "touchy-feely". Nooka always encouraged tiny Alba to explore the world with her hands. They were a huggy family.

'You are doing very well, Alba. Continue to explore.'

The voice faded into silence, leaving Alba puzzled but at the same time elated by the experience. 'But I haven't told you the answer yet.' Silence.

A little disappointed, Alba rose to leave. As she stood up, the gentle breeze again wafted her hair. On impulse, she bent to pick a daffodil. She held the flower close to her nose, delighting in the scent. Was it her imagination or did this seem stronger than before? Thoughtfully, she brushed away a small smudge of pollen from her nose and went back into the house.

Chapter 3
Inatak Runs Away

Molly paced around her bedroom. Sitting still made her jumpy. The day had arrived for her meeting with Tim. No one knew she was planning to meet him, not even her best friend, Alba. She licked her lips which were a little dry, and swallowed hard. Molly had always ventured outside the family home even when quite tiny. She could not wait to explore the world. Occasionally, she had worried her parents by her wanderings. They spoke to her firmly about not talking to strangers, not accepting lifts, all the usual stuff. Molly took all of this in and mostly obeyed.

There were some lapses. She got a lift home from school a few months ago from a man who lived on their street. Although her parents did not know him, Molly thought that since he lived nearby and was seen frequently, it would be OK. At the time, it was raining hard and she had just missed the bus home. As it turned out the trip was reasonably pleasant. Molly regarded herself as a "people person", a grown-up description that Molly related to. The man chatted amiably about his work at the local supermarket and his enthusiasm for his allotment. Molly kept this a secret. She knew her parents would be furious.

Like Alba, Molly was an only child. Maybe this was one of the reasons they got on so well. Molly's mother and father ran a small business which took up a great deal of time. They ran it together, unable to afford assistance. This inevitably meant long tiring days. They were devoted to Molly and it troubled both of them that they were not always there for her. Family time was precious and they all made the most of it but Molly's parents wished they could give Molly much more focused attention. Frequently, they had to miss a parents' evening which added to their feelings of guilt. Molly's schoolwork was consistently good, however. This was evident from her excellent reports.

Molly would like to have had more holidays. Her friends constantly regaled her with exciting descriptions of family holidays abroad. There were several countries Molly wanted to visit but she accepted that for the time being at least, she needed to be patient. Her parents worked very hard most of the years and money was fairly short. Molly's father had plans for a big holiday but it needed to wait for a couple of years.

Molly dressed carefully. She wanted to impress Tim but at the same time, she wanted to appear used to meeting up with boys. She decided on jeans, t-shirt and a smart jacket she'd had as a birthday present. Her hair was loose; her blonde hair framing her face. She had asked her mother to trim her unruly curls, deciding to have a shorter hairstyle. Fortunately, Molly's mother was not only able to dressmake, she could trim her husband and daughter's hair very well.

Pleased with the result, Molly turned from the mirror and picked up her bag, ready to go. The buses still ran frequently on a Saturday. Tim had told her the number of the bus she needed to catch. She also had the map Tim had provided that would lead her to the special meeting place. Molly was pleased and impressed with the way Tim had planned their first meeting.

As she made her way out of the house, she paused before locking the door. Her parents were at work and would not be home until at least six p.m. There was plenty of time for her to meet with Tim and be back home in time. Molly stood for a moment on the doorstep feeling some misgivings. She was not really breaking the rules, was she? After all, Tim was a boy she knew—or just about. Not some random stranger. Nonetheless, Molly felt a twinge of guilt as she made her way down the street. Should she have left a note? Swinging her bag, she quickened her steps. She could just see her bus approaching.

***

Spring sounds and colours were vibrant and abundant as Nooka strolled in the forest. She revelled in her freedom to walk, run or sit wherever she chose. No restrictions here, unlike school where there was no freedom of any kind. Nooka smiled, skipping a little, reminding herself to banish all thoughts of that place. The forest was awakening after the long winter sleep; Nooka paused and listened carefully to the various sounds. The bears were also awakening, reminding Nooka to be vigilant on her walk. She never felt afraid in the forest. But she knew that coming across a bear suddenly could be dangerous. Bears did not react well to being surprised. So Nooka always made some sounds as she walked. Sometimes, she sang the old songs of her people as she wandered through her favourite domain.

As usual, she was making for her special place near the stream. Perhaps now she might find some early watercress to gather for her mother. A rustling sound nearby caused Nooka to stop suddenly. Could it be a bear nearby in the undergrowth? She could not see anything but that did not mean it was not there. It would certainly see her first.

Nooka looked carefully around on hearing a tiny cry. To Nooka's ears, it sounded human, not animal. She had keen hearing, and was able to identify most sounds of the forest and its inhabitants. It was a little early for bear cubs so Nooka cautiously made her way to where the sounds appeared to be coming from. The cry was now a steady whimpering and seemed to emanate from a large bush to the right of the path.

Nooka gently reached out to draw aside the leaves. A small, brown, tearful face gazed up at her.

'Inatak?' Nooka recognised the small boy crouching there trembling, the tears tracking down his dirty face. 'What are you doing here?' Nooka asked, holding out her arms and gently pulling the child out of the bush. He was very dirty, hair matted, his little shirt torn. Nooka held out her arms as he stumbled into them, sobbing.

Nooka gently held him. Inatak was about seven years old. He should not have been in the forest on his own. Nooka took the trembling child's hand. 'Don't be afraid, come with me.'

Hesitantly, he looked up at Nooka's face. 'Where?'

Nooka smiled. 'I shall take you to my special place where we can talk. No one else will be there, it's quite safe.'

When they arrived at the stream, Nooka sat the little boy down on the bank and gently bathed his dirty tear-stained face. She gave him some fruit which she always carried on her forest days. Inatak stuffed it hungrily into his mouth. Clearly the child had been in the forest for hours at least, Nooka thought, looking at the state of him.

Slowly, haltingly, Inatak told Nooka he was running away from home. A few days ago, his brother Tahoma had been taken away to live with another family, a white family, and he would never come back. Nooka listened, horrified. She knew that children were being taken away to residential schools but she had not heard of this. Later, she learned that many tribal children were being put up for adoption to white families.

Nooka held the little boy as he described how his mother had pleaded with the woman who came to take their son. He told Nooka he had never seen his mother cry like that ever. Then came the really bad thing. Inatak began to sob pitifully. 'The bad lady will come for me too when I'm a bit older.'

Nooka sighed heavily. No wonder the poor child had run to the forest. She would return Inatak to his parents but she would ask her father, a tribal elder, if he could help the family. Surely something could be done.

***

'Alba, breakfast's ready,' her mother called from the kitchen.

Alba turned over sleepily. Monday morning already. Sunday had been a pleasant day for the family. Her father had seemed more relaxed, enjoying the spring sunshine. Camille had prepared a picnic with some of the foods that Alba loved. Her mother introduced some interesting dishes to her family. Nooka had given her daughter all her recipes. The family ate a delightful mix of British, French and native dishes.

Nooka's people became known as First Nations. Alba liked that title. After all, her grandmother's people were the first Canadians. During the long relaxing day spent in the nearby countryside, Alba's thoughts turned to her experience in the garden. Had she imagined the whole thing, she wondered. Did she really hear a voice speaking to her as she sat upon the stone?

Alba lay down on the grass, resting her head on her backpack. Closing her eyes, she thought back to the encounter. The voice sounded like a woman's voice, quite a young woman. It had a light, almost tinkling quality that felt rather comforting. Alba thought of the sounds a little waterfall makes. Although the voice could be clearly heard, Alba could not see anyone. Then she remembered she had a fleeting, hazy impression of someone standing near her before the voice began. The figure was so faint that Alba thought it was probably some trick of the light. It was a very sunny day.

She tried to focus on the details. The lady, as Alba now thought of her, spoke to her about flowers. She remembered looking carefully at the daffodils and being asked to see them and smell them in a special way. The voice explained how Alba had five physical senses and that this was the way she related to the physical world. She asked Alba to close her eyes and imagine the sight and smell of the flower. This was quite hard. The lady seemed to give her homework to do on her senses, then she went away.

Alba raised herself to a sitting position. Had she just imagined the whole thing? Still, it was interesting. Maybe she would practice using her senses just to see what might happen.

At that moment, a thrush began to sing in the tree above her head. Immediately, Alba found herself becoming very still and focusing on the bird's song. The notes were pure and beautiful. Alba felt she had experienced something special, that she had listened to the song in a different way. Alba resolved to ask about this if she met the Lady of the Flowers again. Somehow, she felt that there would be another opportunity.

At school that morning, Alba noticed that Molly appeared very subdued. Normally, her friend was bubbly and chatty, keen to engage Alba in conversation at break time. On this occasion, Molly sat quietly at the far end of the playground, listlessly picking at a piece of fruit flapjack.

Alba approached her friend carefully. Sometimes, Molly could be snappy if she was in one of her moods. This time, however, Molly looked up, giving Alba a weak smile.

'Hi, are you all right?' Alba asked. 'You seem a bit quiet today.'

Her friend sighed. 'I'm an idiot, Alba. On Saturday, I was supposed to meet Tim for the first time. I caught the right bus according to Tim's instructions. I looked great as well. Anyway, I was searching in my bag for a packet of crisps and stuff fell out all over the floor. There was an open window and a lot of things got blown about under the seats, including bits of paper. When the bus came to the place where I was supposed to get off, I could not find the map Tim had given me. I had to get off, then catch another bus home. I feel such a fool, Alba. I don't think Tim will bother with me now,' Molly said glumly.

Alba sat down next to her friend. She wasn't quite sure what to say. When Molly first told her about the chat room, she felt uncomfortable with the idea. Then Molly met Tim on the chat room and he seemed nice. Alba thought then that she might have been mistaken. Now, however, listening to Molly, she again felt uncomfortable, even a bit anxious. Alba did not really understand her anxiety about her friend. Then again, she knew that she had a tendency to sense certain things about people. 'There was that word again, "sense". Alba remembered the Lady of the Flowers speaking to her about her senses. She must remember to ask her about this.

Molly nudged her sharply. 'Are you listening to me? I don't think Tim will ask me again.'

'Erm… sorry. I don't know, Molly. But maybe it might be better this way,' said Alba.

Molly stood abruptly. 'Well, you're no help anyway!'

Alba sighed as her friend marched away. When Molly got very cross, her fair skin became quite red. Alba sighed again, collected her bag and went in for her next lesson.

Molly fumed as she entered Mr Khan's chemistry lesson. She was five minutes late. Banging the door behind her, she stormed over to her seat.

'That's not the way to enter my classroom, is it, Molly?' Mr Khan said mildly. He noticed Molly's flushed face. 'OK, well, just remember next time, all right?'

Molly nodded, ruffling the pages of the book on her desk. She found it difficult to concentrate. Usually, she enjoyed chemistry. Mr Khan always made his lessons interesting and engaging for his pupils. Still, she could not stop thinking about her failed trip to meet Tim. What made matters worse was Alba's response to her disappointment. Normally, Alba tried hard to be on Molly's side and to make useful suggestions. This was one of the reasons Molly liked her friend so much. Alba really listened to Molly and seemed to care. This time, she did not seem to be bothered that Molly really wanted to see Tim. In fact, Alba thought that it was not a great idea.

Mr Khan was carefully explaining a practical experiment that all the class would try towards the end of that morning. Molly tuned out, turning her thoughts again to Tim. He was so good-looking; maybe he had already got another girlfriend. Mr Khan turned to write on the board. Molly immediately reached into her bag. She would send Tim a text suggesting another meeting. Lifting her open chemistry textbook to hide her face, she began tapping on her phone.

'Molly Cookson!' Mr Khan, normally a quiet man, spoke loudly and sharply.

Molly's classmates all turned to look. Molly desperately tried to stuff her phone back in her bag. 'Come here and give me that!' demanded Mr Khan.

Molly handed over her phone reluctantly. 'But, sir… I…'

'No excuses, Molly. Not only were you not paying attention, but you know you are not supposed to bring your phone into class,' said Mr Khan firmly.

Molly clenched her fists and took an angry step toward her teacher. 'It's mine, give it back! You can't take it!' shouted Molly.

There was a collective gasp in the room. Everyone's attention was firmly fixed on this exciting development. Mr Khan stood looking at Molly. He said nothing for perhaps a minute. Molly took a step back, her eyes pricking with angry tears.

'I'm surprised at you, Molly,' said Mr Khan quietly. 'Detention this afternoon. Now sit down!'

'But sir, my phone,' Molly pleaded.

'Will be returned to you after detention,' replied Mr Khan, raising his voice. 'Now sit down!' he said sharply.

Molly sulked her way through the day's remaining lessons, her mood dark at the prospect of detention later on. Finally, she was handed her phone, after being firmly reminded to hand it in each morning as per the rules.

This time, when Molly got home, her parents were already back from work. Sometimes, they both worked till early evening. Even if Molly was a bit late home after school, they were usually unaware of this. Sullenly, Molly had to explain her detention and of course got another telling-off from her parents. They were not happy about Molly returning to an empty house on some afternoons.

However, their next-door neighbour was very good, and kept an eye on her. But even so, it was not an ideal situation. When Molly went upstairs to her room, her parents discussed once again the need to make changes. They resolved to try to revise their work schedule.

Upstairs, Molly was also making plans. She carefully put together a text to send to Tim. This time, she apologised for not meeting him as arranged and explained the unfortunate business of the lost map. She stressed how keen she was to meet again as soon as possible. This time, she would make sure she arrived on time at the meeting place. She added that she would be free the following Saturday. Hoping that she had worded the message correctly and that Tim would know how much she really wanted to see him, she sent the text. She went to bed that night with renewed determination to plan everything carefully for next Saturday. *'This time, it will be great,'* thought Molly, feeling pleased with herself.

***

Alba's mother was preparing the evening meal. 'Do you need any help, Mum?' asked Alba.

'No love, everything's under control,' replied Camille.

There was time for Alba to go into the garden and return to the stone seat. She was still wondering if she had imagined everything, but thought she would go and find out. If nothing happened and there was no lady, then Alba would know she had imagined the whole thing. She found the thought of nothing happening very disappointing. The last time helped her when she was feeling so sad about Nooka. The lady's words were comforting.

Although it was early evening, the sun was shining and the large stone was quite warm to the touch. Alba looked around carefully then sat down. *'What should I do now?'* she pondered. *'Perhaps I should close my eyes and just wait. Or,'* she quickly thought, *'I could look at the flowers again.'*

Alba rested her gaze upon a daffodil again, since that was the flower the lady had talked about. She tried to relax. The more she focused on the flower, the more relaxed she felt. A faint sigh—or was it the wind? Alba sensed stillness again and the impression of a presence near her. Again, the sense of a young woman. *'I'm imagining this, of course,'* she thought to herself.

A soft laugh. 'But of course, you are, Alba. Without your imagination, you would find it difficult to know that I am here.'

Alba sat up straight, listening intently. 'You mean I'm not making this up?'

Again, there came a soft laugh. 'Well, yes and no.'

Alba blinked, looking around her with a puzzled expression. 'I don't understand.'

'That is good, Alba, because I think now you do wish to understand. Is this not so?' asked the lady.

'Yes, yes,' replied Alba quickly. 'I really want to know, please.'

A moment of quiet, then the lady spoke again. Alba focused intently on listening to the soft, gentle voice.

'You will recall how I described your five physical senses and how you use them to relate to the world?'

'Yes,' responded Alba. 'I wanted to ask you about the way I seem to feel or think about people. It's like I sometimes pick up things about them. Like when someone is sad. I kind of know they are, without them saying anything.'

'Very good, Alba. This is what we call the sixth sense.'

'I have a sixth sense as well?' asked Alba excitedly.

'We shall come to that. First, I wish to talk a little about your gift of imagination.'

'Oh, I didn't realise it was a gift,' said Alba. 'I mean we all have it, don't we?'

The lady continued. 'That is true. Imagination is being able to "image in". You can create images in your mind, for example. Do you remember I asked you to think of the sight and smell of the daffodil?'

'Yes,' replied Alba eagerly. 'It was easier to imagine seeing it than smelling it.' Alba had the impression that the lady might be smiling.

'Indeed, you remembered this well, Alba. Imagination allows you to build pictures in your mind. You can create and build with thought. This is what I mean by "image in".' Alba nodded thoughtfully. 'It is also a great gift because it is a very creative part of you, and you can develop it,' said the lady.

'How can I do that?' asked Alba.

'What do you love to do, Alba?'

'Immediately, Alba cried, 'Acting! I love to act. I want to be an actor when I grow up.'

'Ah!' replied the lady. 'This is a good example of using your gift of imagination.'

'I'm going to play Harriet in 'Lost at Sea'. This is a play we are doing at school. How do I act her really well?' asked Alba.

The lady went on, 'To be able to really use your gift of imagination well, you need to train it.'

'Like training a puppy?' said Alba.

'Well, not quite. In this case, it means building a picture in your mind of the character in your play, how you think she looks and dresses. How she speaks and what she might be like as a person. This exercise is called visualisation,' the lady explained.

Alba thought this very interesting. She was sure she could visualise Harriet in her mind.

'The next step, Alba,' continued the lady, 'is to visualise yourself playing the part. You see now perhaps how you are training your creative imagination.'

Alba felt very excited. She would definitely start doing this. 'Thank you. Can I ask...' she began.

'Come again tomorrow and we shall continue then.'

The lady's voice faded and Alba realised she had gone. Dusk was approaching as she made her way inside, her head full of the amazing conversation that had taken place. She resolved to make a start with her training this very evening.

Getting ready for bed, Alba remembered her classmate's recent comments about her colour. She winced as she recalled their giggles about her playing fair-haired Harriet. For a moment, she wondered if they were right. Perhaps she was not suitable. *'But Miss Jenkins chose me to play the part,'* she thought *'so she must believe that I can do it.'* As she lay in bed, she imagined herself on stage playing the role she so much wanted. Smiling to herself, she fell soundly asleep.

Chapter 4
Alba to the Rescue

Nooka sat disconsolately on a stool in front of her family home. Like all the village houses, it was a simple one-storey building. Nooka's father was a tribal elder and owned his own fishing boat, so the family were relatively well off. Their house was freshly painted and it had its own small garden. Nooka loved to help her mother sow flower seeds and spent many happy hours sitting near the flowerbed breathing in the scented air.

Inatak had run away again. Fortunately, this time Nooka found him quickly. He had hidden under the same bush. Although Nooka's father had tried his best, the Indian Affairs social worker refused to agree that the child could remain at home. Inatak's family were a little poorer than most of the other villagers. Inatak's father was a fisherman and also did other seasonal work. Even though he worked long hours, sometimes miles away from the village, his pay was meagre. Inatak's mother was not well, and was unable to work. In addition, the loss of her eldest son, Tahoma, had resulted in her falling into a deep depression. Her two sons had habitually spent a lot of time with other families, sometimes not returning home to sleep. This was not unusual in tribal culture for children to stay with a relative or other neighbours. The boys were well looked-after and healthy.

However, this was not what the visiting social worker wished to see. To her, the situation was not acceptable. The father was frequently away, mother not capable and the children were running wild. Inatak's brother had been taken away within days from the family, despite protests by the band council.

Nooka sighed deeply and rose to enter the house, where her mother was preparing dishes for the forthcoming powwow. This was something the entire village took part in. There would be drumming, dancing and feasting. This joyful celebration of their culture was an opportunity to wear their traditional clothes and headdresses. It was a time to celebrate the earth, which was sacred to them. Like most native people, they regarded themselves as stewards of the land, not owners. Nooka had learned from an early age to respect every aspect of the natural world and to care for it as all things are connected.

Out of the corner of her eye, Nooka glimpsed a dark-haired young man walking toward her father and a small group of men. Her heart gave a little jump as she recognised Pierre, the young logger whom she had met the other day. She watched curiously as the young man began to speak to her father.

***

Alba woke bright and early. She had time to go for a quick bike ride before school. Slipping on her shorts and t-shirt, she quietly went through the house to collect her bike from the shed. She set off cycling steadily down the road. There were few cars about at that time of the morning. Approaching the junction at the end of the street, she heard a voice calling, 'Willow, where are you? Willow, Willow?' Alfie, a boy in Alba's class, was standing by his garden gate looking anxious.

Alba drew to a stop. 'What's up, Alfie. Who's Willow?'

'She's my cat. Actually, she's still a kitten, and she's gone missing.'

'Oh dear,' said Alba. 'How long has she been gone?'

'Yesterday and last night,' sighed the boy. 'We've been looking everywhere.'

Alba regarded him sympathetically. 'I could keep a lookout now on my ride.'

Alfie looked at her gratefully. 'Thanks, Alba. Willow, Willow!' he called again.

Alba decided to turn right instead of left at the junction just for a change. She had cycled down Briars Lane past the Holly's farm. Thinking about the missing kitten, she rode slowly looking at each side of the lane and the thick hedges. Apart from birds fluttering in and out of their hedgerow nests, she saw no sign of movement. She approached the farm carefully, as the lane went through part of Mr Holly's farmyard. A small group of hens clucked gently, as they picked out bits of grain. Cows in the nearby large shed were munching steadily, their hot steamy breath visible in the morning air.

Alba was on the far side of the yard, about to resume her ride, when she paused and stopped. She noticed a small shed just beyond the gate in the field nearby. Alba felt one of her strange feelings again. Something seemed to be pulling her towards the shed. Dismounting, she made her way through the open gate towards it. Alba was nearly at the ramshackle old place when she heard a sound. She listened and it came again; a tiny mewing from inside the shed. Alba tried to look through the window but could see nothing through the dirty pane. She tapped gently on the window. Again, came the tiny mew. '*Maybe it's one of Mr Holly's cats,*' she thought. '*Most farms have lots of cats.*' However, since Alfie's cat was missing, she had to find out.

The heavy shed door was difficult to open. Rusty old hinges creaked as Alba gingerly prised it open a few inches. She put her head round the door, seeing old sacks, a few barrels, logs and a couple of large containers in the dimly lit interior. The mewing sound came again, louder this time. Alba managed to squeeze through until she stood in the middle of the shed. She decided to call out the cat's name. 'Willow. Willow.' Alba kept her voice low; she did not want to frighten her.

There was a faint scratching sound coming from one of the large containers in the corner. Alba knelt down carefully, avoiding some rusty old nails. The container was quite long and narrow, with a small opening at the front. Alba peered in but could see nothing. Then a definite loud mewing sound came from the interior. The narrow opening was big enough for Alba to put her arm in, but not very far. She reached in. 'Willow, Willow,' she called again. She could feel nothing. The kitten was probably nearer the back of the container somewhere.

Alba sat back on her heels. Obviously, the cat had crawled in, but for some reason had been unable to get out. Alba's next-door neighbour, who owned a fluffy cat, said cats were inclined to get locked in sheds or garages by accident. Alba stretched her arm as far as she could into the container, calling Willow's name and wiggling her fingers. The mewing was constant now; obviously the poor little thing was very distressed. She would be hungry as well as frightened, stuck there in the dark.

Stumped, Alba pulled her arm out, yelping as she caught her wrist on a sharp piece of metal. The cries were becoming fainter. Alba felt that Willow was becoming weaker. She worried that being stuck inside a container, maybe for many hours, may have harmed the kitten. Alba thought hard. *'I've got to get her out now. If I go to get help, she might get worse in the meantime. What can I do?'* she questioned herself frantically.

In that moment, she remembered the Lady of the Flowers telling her about the importance of the imagination, how creative it was. What would happen if she imagined rescuing the kitten? She thought again, *'What if I imagine I can talk to Willow? Then she would understand she needed to crawl out toward my voice.'* Alba's shoulder slumped. *'What if I haven't done enough training of my imagination?'*

The faint weakening cries began again. Alba knelt, putting her arm through the narrow opening. She closed her eyes, concentrating as hard as she could on the trapped little creature inside. In her mind's eye, she imagined speaking to the kitten. Then she imagined seeing Willow coming toward her outstretched hand. Alba focused as hard as she could on her words communicating with the animal. Then she put her mouth near to the opening, calling softly, 'Willow, come to my hand. Come to my hand.'

Minutes passed, but Alba stayed in that position, arm stiff and aching, her fingers stretched out hopefully. 'Oh dear,' sighed Alba. 'I don't think that worked. Oh!' A small wet nose nudged Alba's little finger, then a warm head moved slowly into her outstretched hand. Alba gasped, heart in her mouth as she felt Willow's little collar under her fingers. Very gently, she grasped the kitten, carefully drawing her out through the container and into the safety of Alba's waiting arms. Alba cried as she cuddled the trembling kitten. 'You're safe now, Willow, you're safe!'

***

Molly and Alba sat together eating their lunch. It was Friday and both were looking forward to the weekend for different reasons. Alba had been invited to Alfie's house on Saturday for tea. The return of Willow to her grateful family still made Alba smile with pleasure. She had walked back from the shed, carefully cradling the kitten under one arm, wheeling her bike. As she reached the house where Alfie lived, she saw him pacing about the garden frowning. Alba rested her bike against the kerb. Holding Willow in her hands, she walked towards him. Alfie's mouth dropped open.

'Ooooh!' He grinned and reached out for Willow. They both went inside to be greeted with cries of relief from Alfie's parents. Willow hungrily devoured her first meal for hours, watched by smiling faces. Alba cycled home having agreed to come to tea on Saturday.

Molly's thoughts were focused on Saturday morning and her meeting with Tim. He had given her the number and time of the bus as before, but this time, she had more information. He had been very pleased that Molly wanted to try again to meet him. He sent her a picture of a small holiday chalet surrounded by trees. It looked pretty. Tim's parents owned the chalet, so Tim thought this would be a special place to meet. His parents would not be there, as it was not the holiday season. Most of the other chalets would also be empty, so they would have the place to themselves.

'I'm going to meet Tim on Saturday, Alba. He texted me again about where we'll meet,' said Molly. Alba nodded. She was only half-listening to her friend. Molly was always full of plans, but they never seemed to amount to anything. The forthcoming play rehearsal after school was uppermost in Alba's mind. She had worked very hard and was virtually word-perfect. What the lady had told her about imagination and visualisation had helped her a lot as she studied her role.

Generally, Alba took most things seriously, giving the impression she was mature for her years. It was true that if Alba was interested in something, she could really apply herself. She hoped that her talks with the Lady of the Flowers would continue. There were so many things Alba wanted to know. She thought about that coming evening, planning to have a longer meeting with the lady.

'You're not listening to anything I'm saying, are you, Alba!' Molly glared at her friend, snatched up her lunch box and stormed off.

Alba groaned. This was Molly all over. Still, she should have shown a bit more interest in her friend's plans, she supposed. Alba found she had lots to think about at the moment, interesting things. Moments of deep sadness about Nooka were fewer, and she felt more able to think of good memories of her grandmother.

The play rehearsal went well. Most of the children had learned their lines. Miss Jenkins was pleased, giving each child praise and encouragement. Mrs Blair, the home economics teacher, was measuring them all for their costumes. Alba loved every minute of the proceedings. Clearly, she had a talent for acting. Miss Jenkins noted Alba's attention to detail, the way she moved and spoke her lines.

She took the opportunity to speak to Alba at the end of the rehearsal. 'That was very good, Alba. I can see that you have worked hard to perfect your performance. You are really convincing as Harriet,' said Miss Jenkins.

Alba flushed with pleasure. 'I just love doing it, miss. When I'm acting, I don't think of anything else, just being the character.'

Lucy Jenkins smiled. 'You seem to be in good spirits at the moment. I notice you smile and laugh more now, just like your old self.'

Thoughtfully, Alba regarded her teacher. Miss Jenkins had been right when she assured her that thinking about Nooka would be easier as time went by. Alba now found herself much more able to think about her grandmother without it being so painful.

'Keep up the good work,' said Miss Jenkins as she left the rehearsal room.

***

After the evening meal, it was too late for Alba to go out into the garden. She planned to get up early the next morning and resume her conversation with the lady. Alba thought back to her earlier conversation with Molly. She was sorry her friend was upset. She did not want to fall out with Molly. A couple of times that evening, Alba tried to call

Molly but each time she only got voicemail. 'Oh well,' sighed Alba, 'I'll try again tomorrow.'

Molly had heard Alba's messages but she was still sulking from their earlier meeting. She felt cross and hurt with her friend, who seemed not to care about how important Tim was to Molly. She shrugged off these thoughts and turned her attention to the following day. Earlier in the evening, Tim had texted her with final instructions for their meeting on Saturday. He reminded Molly of the route she needed to take and expressed excitement about seeing her at last. Molly grinned at this. Tim also suggested that Molly delete his recent texts; telling her that meeting in the special place should be their secret. Molly hesitated only a moment before pressing the delete button. This was so thrilling; she couldn't wait for tomorrow to arrive.

The plan was for Molly to wait until her parents had left for work before leaving to catch the bus. Molly was confident she could go to the special meeting place, spend time with Tim, and then catch the bus home before her parents got back. Molly briefly felt guilty about this. She knew that she ought to tell her parents where she was going.

'Oh, it will be all right,' Molly assured herself.

Having set out the clothes she would wear, checked the bus timetable and map, she went to bed.

***

Alba was keen to go to the stone seat early on Saturday morning. She had lots of questions for the lady and was eager to learn more. Again, the sun was shining, the morning pleasantly warm. With a feeling of expectancy, Alba approached the stone. She sat down carefully, already alert to the sounds and sights around her. All was quiet except for birdsong.

Alba closed her eyes and began to imagine the lady appearing. Once again, she experienced a sense of stillness as she waited silently.

'Greetings, Alba,' came the soft voice. Alba had the impression of being enfolded by the voice, it was so gentle. 'Shall we continue our conversation?'

'Oh yes, please,' Alba replied eagerly. 'I've been practicing visualisation and training my imagination just as you said I should.' Alba had the impression that the lady smiled.

'What has been the most interesting experience for you since we last talked?' asked the lady.

Alba related the story of Willow's rescue, explaining how she had one of her odd feelings and that this had led her to find the lost kitten. 'That odd feeling is your sixth sense, Alba. As well as your physical senses, you have an extra one. Everyone does,' replied the lady.

'Oh,' said Alba, 'you mean that this extra sense sort of led me to find Willow?'

'Yes, indeed, you had an odd feeling, as you call it, and you acted on it with a good result.'

Alba thought for a moment, wondering why she seemed different from other people in the way she related to the world. As if reading her thoughts, the lady said, 'Everyone has this sense, Alba. It is just more developed in some people than in others.'

Alba nodded thoughtfully. 'I think I have always used this sense but I did not understand what it was.'

'Indeed,' said the lady. 'Have you heard people say they did something intuitively?'

'Oh yes,' Alba replied. 'My mother phoned her friend the other day because she had not heard from her for a while. Mum said she felt something might be wrong with her friend. It turned out that her friend was quite ill. My father told me that Mum was very intuitive.'

The lady continued, 'Intuition is very much about the sixth sense, Alba. It is your inner knowing. Following your intuition usually takes you in the right direction.'

Alba was silent for a minute or so. 'It sounds like you are saying we sort of know it already.'

'Yes, indeed, Alba,' replied the lady delightedly. 'You are a very good pupil.'

'Could I learn to develop my intuition so that it becomes stronger?' enquired Alba.

'Yes, of course,' replied the lady. 'This also involves you increasing your sensitivity.'

'You mean practicing sensing things?' asked Alba.

The lady was silent for a moment. She then continued slowly and clearly. 'Spending time in natural environments is a very good way to develop your sensitivity. Here you have a beautiful garden, perfect for your learning. Now, become aware of the daffodils, Alba. Choose one, and then focus your attention on it. Imagine that you are looking at it but with your sixth sense as well, and tell me what you experience.'

Alba let herself be drawn to one flower. She focused intently on its colour, shape and scent. She was surprised to see something else as she gazed at the daffodil. The air around the flower appeared to shimmer. It seemed to Alba that there was some faint light all around it. She closed her eyes, then looked again. The faint shimmering light was still there. Out of the corner of her eye, Alba saw the hazy outline of the lady. She was smiling.

'Tell me what you have experienced, Alba,' she encouraged gently.

Alba described how vivid the daffodil's yellow petals were, how strong the scent. However, she hesitated about the last part of her experience.

'Go on, Alba,' said the lady.

'Well,' said Alba, 'I think I may have imagined this, but I saw a sort of shimmering light around the edges of the flower.'

'Wonderful, Alba!' exclaimed the lady. 'Your imagination is like a doorway. It allows you to see the flower in this way. All living things have a life force. Some people call it an aura. This is what you are sensing and seeing.'

As Alba listened to the lady's words, she realised something about herself. She had always felt different from other children, and not in a good way. Her odd feelings, as she had come to regard them, had made life puzzling and difficult for her. She had striven to be more like her friends, to be like normal people. However, this had not worked. Trying not to have her "odd feelings" had only made her feel worse. But now, the lady's words had changed the way she felt about herself. Yes, she was different, but different in a good way. Her vivid imagination and sensitivity were gifts, not a flaw in her nature. Alba sighed with relief.

'Thank you, thank you so much.'

The lady was silent but Alba sensed her presence and sensed that she was pleased.

Chapter 5
Molly in Danger

Molly's parents left early for work. They had a long, tiring day ahead of them. Molly took her time dressing, having again chosen clothes that flattered her. She brushed her curly blonde hair, pleased with the effect. Surreptitiously, she went to her parents' room to choose some suitable makeup. Her mother always achieved a great look with her eye makeup. Molly tried her best.

'Hmm. I don't think I've quite got the hang of this. Still, it looks OK. My eyes look bigger.'

Smiling at her reflection, Molly took a final look around her bedroom. Satisfied she had everything she needed, she picked up her new trainers and went downstairs. Sitting on the heavy armchair to put on her trainers, Molly admired her new fabric bag. It was very capacious and easy to sling over her shoulder. Placing the bag near to her on the floor, Molly put on her trainers. Beside her, the bag sagged to one side, causing Molly's phone to slide out under the chair. Without looking, Molly reached down for her bag, slung it over her shoulder and went out of the front door.

The morning was bright and sunny, though a little chilly. As Molly set off to walk the short distance to the bus stop, she donned her sunglasses. These made her feel grownup and sophisticated. '*Tim will be impressed,*' thought Molly.

The bus journey was pleasant this time. Not many people had boarded. Molly chose a seat by a window, holding her bag firmly. This time she would not spill its contents on the floor. As she gazed out of the window, she reminded herself of the detailed plan Tim had given her. The special place was a few miles from where Molly lived. Although she was used to taking buses, this route was unfamiliar, taking her out into the countryside. Molly needed to concentrate on the number of bus stops there were before she reached her destination. Tim told her to watch out for the stop on the opposite side of the road from a large pub called The George.

Molly felt excited. Tim was going to bring a picnic, which they would have in the pretty garden at the back of his parents' chalet. Apparently, there was a table, chairs and large umbrella already set up. Tim was so thoughtful, Molly reflected. Woodland Glade, where the chalet was located, sounded lovely. Apparently, all the chalets nestled in a beautiful glade surrounded by trees. There were lots of little trails dotted about in the extensive woods. Maybe she and Tim could do some exploring.

She closed her eyes, lulled by the steady motion of the bus, and fell asleep. A passing motorist sounding a horn woke Molly up with a start. *'On no, please don't let me miss my stop!'* Molly sat up straight, looking out of the window. There was The George pub, just coming into view now. Sighing with relief, Molly grasped her bag and rose from her seat. No one else got off the bus.

She stood for a moment as it drove away. 'Now, there should be a sign for the chalet holiday place not far from here,' said Molly to herself.

Sure enough, a little way up the road, she could see it. Quickening her step, she reached the sign just next to a single-track road. "Woodland Glade Holiday Chalets: Private Road".

There was a footpath running alongside the track, which seemed to be the route for motor vehicles. There were certainly a lot of trees in this place. In fact, the wooded area seemed vast. Molly felt a little overawed by the sight, but she set off along the footpath leading to the chalet complex. The path rose quite steeply at one point. After climbing for a few more minutes, Molly reached the top of a hill. From there, she could see the Woodland Glade site down below her.

All the chalets were clustered together in a glade, surrounded on all sides by thick woodland.

Molly could see ten chalets and what looked like a small shop cum restaurant on the site. She noticed a play area with swings, a sandpit and climbing frame. As she looked down, she thought she heard a car door slam. Tim was coming by bus, and anyway, he was too young to drive.

'Look for the chalet with the yellow front door,' Tim had instructed. 'That's my parents' place. We'll have it to ourselves because it is out of season.'

Molly looked for the chalet with the yellow door. Fortunately, she had excellent eyesight and could see things a long way off. Then she saw it. Tim's chalet was situated in the centre of the ten chalets. It was helpful to know about the yellow door because all the chalets looked the same. Just as Molly prepared to take the steep path down to the site, she saw something quite unexpected. At the far side of Tim's chalet, she could see the rear end of a large black SUV with the boot open. Puzzled, Molly stared at the vehicle. Clearly, the car could not belong to Tim, or to his parents, who were away.

As she watched, a figure came into view. A man seemed to peer closely into the boot of the car, then close it quietly. He stood looking around. Molly could see him clearly. He was fairly short and thin. He had sandy coloured short hair and a wispy beard, which he was now stroking, as he stared in the direction of the site entrance. Molly jumped back behind the nearest tree. Had he seen her? He seemed to be looking straight at her. Peeping round the huge tree trunk, Molly studied him again. Clearly, he was expecting somebody or something.

Tightening her lip, she grimaced. *'This is not Tim. I don't know who this is, but I'm not staying to find out.'* Scared now, Molly edged out from behind a tree, intending to retrace her steps back to the road and safety. As she looked back, she realised the area was dotted with hiking trails. These presumably enabled holidaymakers to explore the beautiful woods at their leisure. Now which one had Molly taken when she left the main road? She glanced back to the chalet nervously. The man looked around again, then disappeared through the yellow front door.

Molly's heart was thumping now, her fear increasing. She knew she must get far away from the place and the strange man. Quickly, she turned and ran along the narrow trail, breathing heavily in her effort to put distance between her and the man. Although he had gone inside the chalet, Molly worried that he might come looking for her. She now felt certain this was some kind of trap, that Tim had tricked her.

'Who is Tim really?' she questioned. After all, she had only communicated with him on her phone

and he seemed so nice. Molly felt a mix of fear and shame. She knew she had been impulsive and stupid.

She urged herself on, racing along the trail, feeling increasing panic with every stride, not knowing she had missed the way out of the site. In her haste to leave, she had chosen a trail that was leading her deep into the woods. Molly came to a sharp turn. Without pausing, she rushed round the bend. Suddenly, she was winded, as she fell heavily on top of a large tree branch lying across the trail. Sprawling full length across the obstruction, she hurt herself badly. Blood tricked from a cut on the side of her head. Her chest heaved painfully as she tried to regain her breath.

She was in shock for a few moments, not quite knowing which bits of her body she had hurt. Raising her head made her feel dizzy and a bit sick, so she lowered it again. Using both hands she tried to push herself up. Again, the wave of dizziness and nausea. Trying again slowly, she managed to lever herself up a little, so that both hands were firmly placed on the branch. So far so good. She tried to get onto her knees, yelping as a sharp pain shot through her right leg. Gingerly, she turned her head to look behind her. She had fallen heavily and awkwardly, catching her right foot under the branch as she fell.

Molly took a deep breath, though it hurt her chest, managing to change her position a little. Gasping with pain, she put all her weight on her left side, so she could pull her right leg out. She cried out as she made the movement, her foot still stuck. Molly lay down across the branch again and vomited.

***

The village was quiet. Most of the families had returned to their homes after the Powwow. Nooka strolled a little way along the path that led toward the forest. She looked up at the night sky. There were so many stars that Nooka could see on this clear night. It seemed to her they were above her, beside her and all around her. Whenever Nooka saw the stars like this, any worries or fears left her. She stood still, gazing with wonder at the beauty surrounding her.

A soft movement behind her alerted Nooka. She was always aware of the possibility of a black bear wandering into the village, searching for food. She turned slowly; it was the young man, Pierre. He was smiling at her. '*Bonsoir.* Good evening, *mademoiselle.* I was hoping that I would see you again.' Nooka flushed with pleasure. Earlier, when she noticed Pierre speaking to her father, she hoped that he would approach her again.

'I was just looking at the stars,' she said shyly. 'They are beautiful.'

'Like you if I may say,' responded Pierre. The two stood together quietly, at ease in each other's presence.

'I was speaking to your father about the possibility of acquiring a fishing boat,' said Pierre. 'Although I'm doing logging for a living now, I want to fish. I thought that the best way to start would be to come to your village of experienced fishermen.'

Nooka was pleased. She was very proud of her father. 'Will he help you?' she asked.

Pierre smiled. 'Yes, indeed. He has already got in mind an old fishing boat in some need of repair. He plans to help me with this.'

Nooka felt excited by this news. It meant she would see much more of Pierre. At sixteen, she was close to leaving the school at last. She shuddered at the thought of that dreadful place. Pierre looked concerned.

'Are you all right, Nooka? Your name is Nooka, isn't it?' Nooka had turned pale, so the young man took her hand gently. 'Is something wrong? Perhaps, I can help.'

Everything tumbled out at once; Nooka's own horrible experiences at the school and other village children being sent away to residential schools. She began to sob, as she described the terrible suffering of many children. Neighbouring villages all had sorrowful tales to tell. There were families whose children had been so cruelly abused that they died. Sometimes, the families never knew what had happened to them. Nooka told Pierre how some of the children developed hearts of stone as a way of coping.

Pierre listened to this with growing horror. 'I had no idea it was as bad as this. I'm from Quebec, so I did not know what went on over here,' explained Pierre. 'You see, I was born and brought up in Montreal. My parents wanted me to go to university and become a doctor like my father, but I did not want that. I love the outdoors and I also love to travel. I wanted to explore our amazing country. When I arrived here, I found work as a logger. You see, Nooka, I'm also really interested in learning about other people and their cultures.'

Carefully, Pierre led the sobbing girl to a nearby log and sat her down. 'I am glad that your time at the school is nearly over,' he said gently. 'But will you be all right in these last months?'

Nooka nodded, wiping her eyes on her sleeve. 'Yes, I think so. Now I know how to keep out of the masters' way and to avoid angering them as far as possible. My English has improved,' she added ruefully.

'Is there anything I can do to help?' asked Pierre.

Nooka wondered if he might be able to do something to help Inatak and his family. So far, her father and the others of the band council had failed to move the social worker. Inatak could be taken at any time. The family were increasingly desperate. Any help at all would be good now. Pierre listened carefully, unsure whether the social worker would listen to him. However, he would surely try his best to help the little boy and his family.

***

The trickle of blood from Molly's temple had stopped but she still had waves of dizziness. This time, she would try another manoeuvre to free her foot. Lifting as much of her body as she could away from the heavy branch, she pushed it as hard as she could. Fortunately, the branch shifted just enough for Molly to prise her foot out.

Gasping with exertion and pain, Molly pulled herself into a sitting position. She leaned against the large trunk of a tree close to the trail. Molly sat for several minutes, still breathing heavily. The dizziness was wearing off a little, but she still felt nauseous. Worse though was her right ankle. Even with her socks on, she could see how it was rapidly swelling. Touching it gently, she winced with pain. Doubting her ankle would take her weight, she reached for her bag. Luckily, it was within reach.

Relieved, she reached inside for her phone. Her parents would be at work and they would be furious with her. Molly sighed, then went rigid with shock. She could not find her phone. Panicking, she tipped out all the contents. It was not there. Molly put her head in her hands and sobbed bitterly. What an idiot she had been! And now, here she was completely stuck in a strange wood. For several minutes, she wept with the pain and her foolishness. Deep down, she admitted to herself she had made a big mistake with Tim.

It was not as if she had not been warned about contacting strangers on the Internet. They had regular advice in school from the teachers. Molly's parents would have been horrified by her behaviour. She dreaded to think who that man was in the chalet. Molly stopped crying at once. She ought to find somewhere she could hide in case he came looking for her.

Getting on her hands and knees, Molly crawled a few yards from the trail. Her ankle hurt furiously but Molly gritted her teeth. Walking was not an option. Just putting her foot on the ground and pressing a little made her gasp with pain. Lifting her head, she noticed a dense copse some way ahead and slightly up the hill. There were no buildings in sight, only the occasional bench for walkers. The trees might give her some shelter and protection.

Looking at her watch, Molly saw that it was later than she thought. She must have taken more time on the bus, apart from all the blundering about since she arrived. Crawling on her hands and knees was exhausting and painful. Although Molly was very good at sports, and was generally fit, she was finding this very hard. Every few yards, she had to stop and gather her strength.

Eventually, she reached the copse. Several trees were clustered close to one another. All were in full leaf. Molly dragged herself toward a suitable-looking tree with a large trunk and full canopy. Gratefully, she leaned her back against the rough bark. All her muscles were burning from the uphill climb, but she felt safer here, where the trees stood around her protectively. Hopefully, the man would give up whatever he had planned and would go away. Molly shuddered when she thought about what might have happened had she actually got as far as the chalet.

The day was warm, so she removed her jacket, placing it carefully beside her bag. Suddenly, she was aware she was hungry. It was a long time since her breakfast. Although Molly had been expecting a picnic with Tim, she still had a few snacks in her bag. She drew out a bottle of orange juice, a packet of mixed nuts and raisins, a bar of chocolate and some gum; all of which she arranged carefully on the ground. Molly looked at her snacks, tempted to eat everything at once. However, she knew that she must only eat a little now, saving the rest.

She shivered, despite the warmth, when she thought about her situation. No one knew she was here. She had no phone and she could not walk. 'This is not good, Molly,' she said to herself. She was just reaching for the packet of nuts and raisins when she saw a movement.

A small red squirrel was scampering down the tree trunk. It sprang over Molly's shoulder and landed a few feet away, regarding her with its sharp dark little eyes. Molly looked at the pretty little creature with its bushy red tail standing up. She had never seen a red squirrel before, except for a picture in a book. They were quite rare, particularly in this part of the world. Very carefully and slowly, so as not to frighten her new friend, she opened the packet of nuts and raisins. Picking out a little selection of nuts, she scattered them on the ground. The squirrel twitched its tail and leapt toward the nuts, scooping one up in its tiny hands. Molly watched the squirrel delicately eating the nuts, finding it a relaxing distraction. Resting her back against the tree, she fell asleep for the second time.

When she awoke, it was already getting dark. Fortunately, Molly did not feel cold yet, but she feared that that would not be the case if she had to stay there all night. Her ankle throbbed painfully. '*Maybe it's broken,*' thought Molly. '*Or perhaps it's a sprain. Whatever, I can't walk on it.'* Molly wondered if she could hop her way down to the main road. If she had a sturdy stick to hand, it would serve as a crutch. There seemed to be nothing lying on the ground that she could use; only a sprinkling of leaves and a few small twigs. Molly sighed. *'If this were a story, there would be a perfect stick or branch that I could use to get out of here.'*

Tears trickled slowly down Molly's cheeks. She had very little left to eat or drink. Most of the nuts and raisins were gone. Molly gave the squirrel quite a lot. Sharing the food meant company for her, even though she had deprived herself in the process. Molly wondered when she would be missed. Hopefully, when her parents got home, they would search for her. She brightened when she remembered the missing phone. It must have slipped out of her bag before she left home. All her parents had to do was check her messages. Tim's instructions were there. They could easily find her. Molly felt a huge wave of relief. She could be confident of rescue soon.

Suddenly, she sat bolt upright. A horrible thought had struck her. *'I deleted all the texts about my meeting with Tim. He told me to do that.'* Molly's shoulders slumped in defeat. Too late, she realised how cleverly she had been deceived from the beginning. The good-looking fourteen-year-old boy calling himself Tim was really the man she saw at the chalet.

Despite the difficulty of her situation now, things could have been much, much worse. Molly chose not to dwell on what might have happened had she gone to the chalet. It was quite dark now and Molly was beginning to feel cold. She put on her jacket, huddling against the tree trunk for warmth. She listened to the various sounds of the wood at night. Fortunately, Molly was not alarmed by the rustlings of small creatures in the undergrowth or the occasional cry of an owl. Since childhood, Molly's family had camping holidays in the countryside.

Molly groaned. Another horrid thought came to her. She had arranged a sleepover at her friend Sophie's house this Saturday. When they got home, Molly's parents would assume that she was with Sophie. Placing her bag on the ground, she painfully shuffled her body around until she could lie down, using the bag as a pillow. Molly wept, her tears soaking her new bag. However, despite the throbbing in her ankle and her uncomfortable position, Molly eventually fell asleep.

Chapter 6
Inatak and the Bear

On Sunday morning, Alba woke with a start. She had had a disturbing dream about Molly, where Molly was running and shouting for help. Alba lay thinking about her friend, regretting their falling-out the other day. She had tried to call Molly yesterday morning unsuccessfully, and then she was out having tea with Alfie and his parents. Alba had spent a very pleasant afternoon chatting to Alfie and playing with Willow. She was glad to see that the kitten had completely recovered from her misadventure.

Alba returned her thoughts to her friend. She had trepidations before about Molly's plans to meet Tim. Now she was feeling more anxious about her friend. It was still early, and being a Sunday, it was likely that Molly's parents would be having a lie-in. She knew how hard they worked all week. Alba decided to wait a while before calling Molly. The anxious feeling was not going away. Perhaps she should try to speak to the Lady of the Flowers.

Alba went straight to her stone seat. Keen to begin, she started with a question. 'Please can you help me about something?' Silence. Alba asked again. Silence. Confused, Alba looked around her. She could not get any sense of the lady's presence. Perhaps she had gone away, Alba thought. She fidgeted on the seat, feeling quite agitated. 'Hello.' She called. There was no reply. Apart from birdsong and the sound of the occasional passing car, all was silent. Troubled, Alba twisted a strand of her long hair, pulling it sharply. At that moment, she was aware of the phone ringing in the house. Alba sighed and decided to give up trying to contact the lady.

'Alba, Alba,' called her mother, running across the garden. 'Come into the house.' Alba saw that her mother looked pale and worried. She followed her into the kitchen, where her father sat with a concerned expression on his face. Looking at her parents, Alba realised that something was very wrong.

'What is it? What's the matter?' she asked anxiously.

'That was Molly's mother on the phone. Molly did not come home last night. They assumed that she had gone to a sleepover at Sophie's house but she hadn't,' said Camille.

Alba went very still. Her mother bit her lip and shook her head. 'They rang everyone, but no one has seen Molly.' Camille's voice quavered. 'They have called the police.'

Alba's father reached out his arms and Alba went straight to him. He held his daughter, stroking her head. 'Try not to worry too much. The police are out searching for her now.'

Camille regarded her daughter thoughtfully. 'Does Molly have her phone with her all the time?'

'Yes,' replied Alba. 'She gets told off for having it in lessons.'

Her mother frowned. 'She's not picking up. Her parents keep trying to call her.'

Alba listened to this news sombrely, understanding now the reasons for her dream and subsequent anxiety. This was the moment to reveal to her parents all that she knew of Molly's plan to meet Tim. She recounted carefully everything she could remember. Unfortunately, she had not listened to much of what Molly had said. She knew only that Molly was to meet Tim on that Saturday at a special place. Alba remembered Molly receiving texts, but not the contents. She shook her head sadly.

David and Camille looked at their daughter with concern. 'Whatever has happened, it's not your fault,' reassured Camille.

Her father joined in. 'We will contact the police and tell them what you have told us. It may be useful for them.'

Alba left her parents already lifting the phone to make the call. She walked back into the garden, worrying about her friend. She looked at the stone seat at the far end of the garden. Alba then decided to try contacting the lady again. The daffodils around the stone were still in full bloom. She remembered the first time the lady appeared, and the conversation about the flowers. This was her connection to the lady, Alba thought. The daffodils. She arranged herself comfortably on the stone, trying to push away some of the anxiety she was feeling. Composing herself, she focused on one daffodil. At the same time, she imagined the lady being there. A few minutes passed, then a slight breeze crossed Alba's brow.

'Greetings, Alba,' came the soft voice. 'I think you have learned a valuable lesson.' Pleased to have contact again, Alba listened intently. The lady continued. 'The first time you attempted to contact me this morning, you were very agitated and emotional. This made it difficult for you to use your sixth sense. You see, you need to be still and quiet in your mind. You could imagine looking at the white clouds passing in the blue sky if you have worrying thoughts. Each cloud drifting past is like an unwanted thought drifting from your mind.'

Alba liked the idea of the clouds floating past in the sky. *Imagining this would be quite easy,* she thought.

'You have a question,' stated the lady.

For the next few minutes, Alba told her about Molly. Was there anything that Alba could do to help her friend to be found? She sensed the lady's presence strongly. It felt very comforting and also gave her hope.

'Do you remember what led you to find the missing kitten?' asked the lady.

'Oh, yes,' replied Alba. 'I remember taking a different route on my bike ride that day. I usually follow the same route on my ride. I don't know why I did that. Then just coming through Mr Holly's farmyard, I noticed the shed and had one of my odd feelings. I felt quite strongly drawn to look at it.'

The lady continued steadily. 'Were you thinking about Willow on your ride?'

'Yes, I was,' replied Alba.

'So, intuitively, you took a different route and searched a strange shed,' said the lady.

Alba responded quickly. 'Yes, I was using my sixth sense, wasn't I?'

The lady smiled. 'Indeed. You can use that experience to help your friend.'

Alba thought very carefully about this. Perhaps the lady was suggesting that Alba should concentrate on Molly, to allow her sixth sense to work. 'Oh,' said Alba. 'I'm not sure I would be able to do that. After all, I am only learning to do this sort of thing.'

A soft laugh. 'Well, Alba, perhaps this would be a challenge for you and an opportunity to use your gift of imagination. I am helping you to access your own inner wisdom. You know more than you think you know,' the lady said gently.

Alba nodded. 'Thank you. I shall try to remember what you have told me. I am so worried about Molly.' Alba listened but there was nothing more. The lady had gone.

By Sunday afternoon, there was still no news of Molly. Several people in the neighbourhood were out looking. Many of Molly's school friends and their parents joined in the search. Alba chose to stay in her bedroom to see if anything would come to her about her friend. She remembered the lady's advice to be quiet and still before focusing her thoughts on Molly. Alba opened her box full of old toys, books and photos. Several pictures were there of Alba and Molly. They had known each other ever since reception class at primary school. Alba hoped that knowing Molly so well for so long would help her in her task.

***

Molly had spent a very uncomfortable night, curled up upon the hard ground. She was cold and stiff, her ankle hurt all the time. Standing was impossible. She could not bear any weight on her injured foot. Her meagre supplies of food and drink were long gone. Molly's stomach growled with hunger. She was at least thankful it was now light. The long, dark night had seemed never-ending. Molly had never felt so afraid in all her life.

Hours had gone by with no sign of help coming. Surely, her parents had found her phone by now. She hoped that they might be able to retrieve the deleted texts. Molly was not sure that this could be done but they would see the earlier texts from him and his photo. She grimaced at the thought of her previous excitement when Tim first made contact. Well, she was certainly paying for that mistake now, she thought.

Her mouth and lips were so dry, she longed for some water. Being thirsty felt worse than the hunger. As if on cue, the squirrel appeared. Its little nose twitching in anticipation of food. Molly looked at it sadly.

'No more nuts now.'

Instead of scampering off, the squirrel sat down quite near her and began busily cleaning itself. Molly smiled. She was grateful for the company.

The day was warming up now. Molly's stiffness began to wear off a little. She wondered where the people would go looking for her. Woodland Glade was a few miles from her home. She supposed they would mostly concentrate the search near to her home at first. Molly had seen TV news programmes where lots of people spread out in lines, searching fields and so on. Apart from Alba, no one knew about Tim. And because they fell out, Molly did not tell Alba where she was going. She wondered if there would be any people walking in these woods on a Sunday. Then she remembered that the holiday site was private. Really, the only clues to Molly's whereabouts were on her mislaid phone.

Molly sighed. The squirrel had finished washing itself and was looking expectantly at Molly. 'No more nuts,' she repeated. Twitching its bushy red tail, the squirrel ran up Molly's tree. Tired from the discomfort of the previous night, she rested her head on her bag and tried to sleep.

For most of the afternoon, she dozed, changing her position every now and then in an effort to get comfortable. Molly tried not to worry about her ankle, which continued to throb painfully. It hurt so much that Molly concluded it was broken. She looked up into the large canopy of leaves. In a story, she reflected, water would conveniently drip from the leaves into her mouth. She was dreadfully parched now and the nausea had returned. 'What if nobody finds me?' she whimpered. 'I'll die here.'

***

Alba went downstairs to the kitchen to get a drink of orange juice. Her parents were out searching for Molly. So far, nothing had been discovered about her disappearance. The search was now widening with more volunteers joining in. Molly's parents had been advised to stay at home in case their daughter contacted them. A young policewoman stayed with them to lend support. WPC Williams was a kind young woman. She made a point of assuring Molly's parents that the police were being extremely vigilant in their search, and would not give up, however long it took. She also made frequent cups of tea and coffee for them, a small but comforting contribution.

Back upstairs in her bedroom, Alba sat on her bed sighing. So far, despite intense concentration on Molly, nothing had come to mind. On the floor, the contents of her old toy box lay strewn randomly. She listlessly moved them around, seeing another photo of Molly and herself at the zoo when they were six. Alba smiled at the memory of Molly waving and talking to a large orangutang who was holding her baby close. The pair disappeared from view, leaving both girls disappointed. However, something happened then that the girls never forgot. The mother returned, carefully placing the baby on the floor by the window, directly facing Molly and Alba. Both children gasped with delight. It was as though the mother was introducing her baby to them.

Putting the photo to one side, Alba noticed an envelope marked 'Canada'. On opening it, several photos tumbled out. Alba picked out a picture of her mother, father, grandmother and grandfather, smiling against the background of a lake. Alba never knew her grandfather Pierre, who died just before she was born. Although he spent most days on his fishing boat, he agreed on one occasion to help out the loggers. He had worked full-time as a logger years ago, but preferred his work at sea. There was an accident. Pierre was killed instantly by a falling tree-branch. The locals called them widow-makers.

Nooka was devastated by the loss of her beloved Pierre. They had married when Nooka was just seventeen. Pierre learned how to fish from Nooka's father. The whole village had welcomed the young French Canadian into their midst. Clearly, he had shown deep respect for them and their traditions. He was keen to know about their culture, even trying to master their language. Pierre only managed to speak a few words but the villagers loved the fact that he had tried. He became a spokesman for them in their dealing with the Department of Indian Affairs.

Pierre and Nooka lived in the village. When their daughter Camille was born, Pierre made sure she was educated in the village native school and also the school in the nearby town. Alba remembered Nooka telling her that Pierre wanted his daughter to be well-educated.

'You see, Alba, Camille is Métis, which means she is part white and part First Nations. Your grandfather did not want his daughter to face discrimination.'

Alba's mother had explained how First Nations people were not treated well, and that her father encouraged her to be proficient in both English and French, and to study hard at school. Alba felt sad that Nooka's people had such difficult lives. She thought it desperately unfair. Alba had been brought up to respect all people, irrespective of colour or culture.

'Never let your heart turn to stone, Alba.' Nooka had said. Her grandmother was such a loving person, and never bitter. A few tears fell, as Alba again felt the acute loss of her beloved Nooka. She turned back to the photograph of the family. Camille did very well at school, deciding that she wanted to go to university in Montreal, where her father had studied. She chose to major in French. In her second year, she met David, on student exchange from the UK. Together, they frequently travelled to the west coast to visit Nooka and Pierre. These were happy times. Camille loved introducing David to her parents. They married in a small town near their old home and had a special wedding celebration with Nooka, Pierre and the whole village.

Alba carefully placed the photo back in the envelope. The house was quiet, her parents still out searching. Perhaps, the Lady of the Flowers might help with her efforts to find Molly. So far, Alba felt that her sixth sense was not working. Nothing about Molly's whereabouts surfaced in her mind.

Back on the stone seat, Alba took time to relax her body and still her mind. She hoped very much the lady would appear.

'I see you are striving hard to find your friend, Alba,' said the familiar voice.

Relieved, Alba replied, 'I'm so glad you're here. I think I may be doing something wrong, because I still haven't a clue about Molly.'

'You are still learning, child. Do not be so hard on yourself. With this kind of work, you need to take it gently,' she said.

Alba was perplexed. 'I don't know what you mean.'

The lady explained patiently. 'Sometimes, when there is a problem and your mind works very hard to solve it, without rest, your mind becomes tired. That is the time to stop trying.' Alba did not think this made much sense. However, she listened carefully. 'You stop trying and this creates a space in your mind. Then you wait and allow the answer to come,' said the lady.

Alba thought carefully. 'Does that mean that I may have the answer within me, but that it is in a different part of my mind?'

'Good, Alba, this is very encouraging. May I suggest something else that might help you?' asked the lady. Alba nodded. 'Do you have anything that belongs to Molly? It could be something quite small.'

Alba thought about her friend and the many things they had given each other over the years. 'I have,' Alba replied. 'Molly and I swapped bracelets that we had for ages since we were little.'

The lady smiled. 'That would be very suitable. Quite simply, you hold her bracelet and then focus your thoughts on Molly. Remember, the more relaxed you are the better. Then allow thoughts or pictures or feelings to come into your mind.

Alba asked, 'What does the bracelet do?'

The lady explained carefully. 'It simply helps to focus your mind, and allows your intuition to work more freely.'

Alba was keen to return to her bedroom to find Molly's bracelet. She stood up smiling. 'Thank you very much.' Then she hastened back into the house.

***

Inatak's mother was not well again. His father had been away for several weeks now. Quietly, Inatak went outside to fetch his special stick and the old metal tin. He practiced drumming regularly. One day, he hoped to have a real drum. He saw his friend, Koyah, who lived nearby, also practicing. Both boys began happily playing their drums.

After about half an hour, Koyah put down his stick. 'Shall we play climbing trees now?'

Inatak grinned, jumping up to follow Koyah to the trees they climbed many times.

Inatak noticed a car coming up the road towards the village. As it drew nearer, Inatak gasped. It was the bad lady. She had come for him just as she had come for his brother Tahoma. He stood, his knees trembling with fear. He would be taken away to live with a strange white family, and like Tahoma, he would never come back. Inatak saw the bad lady open the car door. She was carrying a pile of papers in her hand. He dodged behind an old truck to watch without her seeing him. With firm, determined strides, the social worker made her way straight to Inatak's house.

He did not wait for his mother to open the door. He turned and fled. Running as fast as he could, he made for the path leading into the forest. He took a brief look back. The lady had gone into his home. Tears streaking his face, Inatak raced towards the stream and the big bush where he had hidden before. He stopped abruptly. Last time he hid there, Nooka found him and brought him back home. He could not hide there again. This time, he must find somewhere he could not be found. The little boy took a deep breath and ran on, heedless of scratches, as he swerved round bushes and trees. When he reached the stream, he bent to drink the clear fresh water. He looked around. There was the big bush he had chosen as his first hiding place. Shaking the water off his hands, he ran on along the bank of the stream, and then turned off sharply when he saw a narrow trail leading further into the forest.

Inatak slowed to a walk now, confident that no one was following him. He found himself in a clearing with high rocks on one side. Could he hide somewhere here, he wondered. While he was searching, he heard little squeals and grunts close by him. Three very young black bear cubs ran into the clearing. They were jumping on each other, play-fighting, having a lovely time. Inatak was horrified. The presence of the cubs meant that their mother would be very close by. One of the cubs came quite near him, looking up at him curiously, seemingly unafraid. Inatak had to act fast. He had to hide. But where? Not up a tree because bears climb trees fast. Frantically, he looked all round him. The only possible place would be the area of large rocks. He studied them for a suitable one that he could climb. When the mother bear returned, she would most likely attack him, so he had to climb high quickly.

The little boy was slightly built, but agile and strong. He chose a large granite rock that towered above him. Although the rock face looked smooth, Inatak could see small indentations where he could place his hands and feet. He was a good climber. He and Tahoma regularly climbed trees together. Carefully, he felt for a place to start, and slowly began his ascent, mindful that mother bear could return any minute. He was careful to steady himself before reaching up for the next cleft in the rock.

He was just over halfway when he heard the bear lumbering through the undergrowth. In seconds, she would be in the clearing. He managed another couple of feet and then she came in. Inatak dared not look round in case he lost his balance. The bear went first to her cubs then, sniffing intently, she turned her great head towards Inatak. Swiftly, she launched her heavy body, slamming it hard against the rock face. Inatak was desperately trying the get himself out of her reach. The sweat was pouring from his head into his eyes, making it hard to see the narrow cleft in the rock above him. The bear slammed against the rock again, growling with anger.

Then, with surprising speed, she reared up on her hind legs, reaching up towards the boy. Inatak's feet were now dangerously close to the bear's sharp claws. Heart thumping, he managed to move his right foot into a cleft. Then he screamed. The bear had swiped his left leg with razor sharp claws, tearing his trousers and gashing his leg. Chest heaving, he pulled himself up with both hands, luckily finding a foothold for his right foot. Just above him was a narrow ledge. Panting with exhaustion, he managed to heave himself onto the ledge.

Below him, the bear was still lashing out, looking up at him through angry little eyes, its hot breath steaming from its wide-open mouth. Inatak lay still, trying to catch his breath. He could feel the blood oozing from his leg, but dared not move to take a look. Below him, the bear dropped down and sat looking up at him. Her cubs were still playing happily. She showed no sign of leaving. Inatak's injured leg hung over the edge. He was unable to lift it. Blood was now streaming from the deep wound, trickling down the side of the granite rock. The bear turned her head, lazily licking a few drops, looking up expectantly at the child. She was going nowhere.

Chapter 7
Alba Takes a Chance

Alba was feeling anxious and frustrated. Time was passing quickly. Molly had not yet been found. So far, Alba had only a faint picture in her mind that connected to Molly. At least Alba hoped there was a connection. She followed the lady's advice, holding Molly's bracelet to help her focus. The little charms dangling from the bracelet had been collected over the years; even when Molly's wrist got too big to wear it. When the girls swapped their bracelets, it marked the strength of their friendship.

Alba decided to write down the information she had, even though it seemed sparse. When she held the bracelet and thought about Molly, she felt afraid. The picture that came to her mind was of Molly running away from a small group of buildings. It was not very clear but they seemed fairly small. There was a narrow road near the buildings. The lady had advised her to pay attention to everything she experienced. Alba sensed her friend must be very frightened. Alba herself was anxious.

She needed to contact her parents to let them know this new information. Alba hoped they would take this seriously. She was determined to do whatever it took to find her best friend. Camille and David would have taken their phones with them on the search. Alba tried twice but each time got their voicemail. She made herself a quick drink and sat in the kitchen wondering what to do and where to go. Joining the search was an option but did not feel right.

Putting her notes carefully in her bag, she decided to cycle over to Molly's parents. She knew they would be there all the time. Perhaps they would listen to her even though they might think that she was making it all up. She resolved to tell them anyway, no matter what they thought of her.

WPC Lisa Williams had just made another pot of tea and was handing round biscuits. Alfie's parents were old friends of the family so they had called in to lend their support. Alba arrived a little out of breath. She had ridden as fast as she could over to Molly's house. The young policewoman came to the door. She smiled, 'May I ask who you are?'

'I'm Alba, Molly's best friend. I'd like to see her parents please,' said Alba, still breathing hard.

The grownups looked surprised to see her. However, Mrs Cookson regarded Alba blankly, her face white and strained.

'We haven't heard anything yet,' said Mr Cookson. 'This young lady is WPC Williams. She's a family liaison officer.'

'I've just made tea and biscuits for everyone,' said WPC Williams. 'Shall I make another cup?'

Alba looked at her gratefully. 'Er… thank you, but not at the moment. 'Actually,' Alba cleared her throat, feeling apprehensive about what she wanted to say to them. Molly's parents were obviously desperately worried and Alba did not know how they would react.

'What is it, Alba?' said Mr Cookson sharply.

Alba stood nervously looking around at the adults. She hesitated then took a deep breath.

'I had a sort of picture about where Molly might be. It just came into my mind,' said Alba. 'I know it might sound strange but I felt that I had to tell you.' The room became very quiet. 'I… er… I…' Alba stammered, going rather pale.

Mr Cookson stood up. 'Really, Alba, don't you think we have enough to worry about without you coming here with your silly stories?' he retorted angrily.

Mortified, Alba turned and rushed out of the room. Just as she was about to open the front door, Alfie's father called out. 'Alba, is this the same kind of thing that led you to find our kitten Willow?'

Unsure, Alba remained standing by the front door. WPC Lisa Williams came over to her. 'I would like to know what you experienced, Alba,' she said quietly.

Alba looked at her with relief. 'You see, I get these odd feelings. That's how I found Willow.'

The young policewoman regarded Alba thoughtfully. 'Can you tell me what you saw?'

Alba described what she had seen as clearly as she could, while Lisa Williams took notes. 'I'm going to call this in,' she said. Alba waited while the policewoman went to speak to the Cooksons. Then they both went outside where Lisa immediately made her call.

'I've reported this, Alba. My colleagues will follow it up. It took some guts to come over and say all this. Good for you.' Alba smiled gratefully. Lisa handed her a card. 'You can contact me on this number at any time. If anything else comes to you, about Molly's whereabouts, give me a call.'

***

By the early evening, Molly was still missing. The police had investigated several clusters of buildings approximating to Alba's description. They searched the local golf club grounds and an old school house with lots of outbuildings. They also looked around building sites and narrow lanes with small groups of single-storey dwellings. Nothing, no sign of Molly. By now, Alba's parents were home, very tired and downhearted. They were not aware of Alba's intervention and further police searches. Alba had just called WPC Williams for an update. She ran to her parents and burst into tears. They sat her down and gently coaxed the story from her.

Alba was very down. She picked at her food, and then went to her room. Slumping down on the bed, she hit one of her pillows with frustration. She felt stupid and useless. Molly was still out there somewhere and Alba had failed her. Not just that, she had probably wasted police time. The light was beginning to fade. In spring, it would not get fully dark for some hours yet. Poor Molly, out alone somewhere facing another night. Alba looked out of her bedroom window. In the half-light, the stone seat at the end of the garden loomed large and mysterious. Disconsolate, she lay down, thinking of the lady's advice.

'*Maybe I just don't have enough experience of this kind of thing,*' she thought.

Despite feeling restless and edgy, Alba found herself drifting towards sleep. As she relaxed, fleeting images came and went. At one point, she thought she heard a voice faintly whispering, 'Trust yourself, Alba, trust yourself.' More strange images came. Quite clearly, she saw a signboard swinging in the wind with the words "Woodland Glade" in large letters. Alba sat up with a start, shaking her head to clear it of any lingering drowsiness.

'Woodland Glade,' she said aloud to herself. Alba knew at that moment that this was an important clue connected to Molly. Indeed, she felt that it was a sign in more ways than one. This was a real place but she had no idea where it was. Perhaps her parents would know.

She rushed downstairs. 'Mum, Dad, I think I might know where Molly is!' she cried. Her parents were having a late evening meal. They looked at their daughter with concern. She had always been a rather dreamy, oversensitive child with a huge imagination. David hesitated before speaking. He did not want to upset her any more than she was already. Molly was his daughter's best friend. They were very close.

'I think it would be best if we leave the matter entirely to the police,' he said gently. 'I'm afraid that because you are so worried, you may be imagining things. Actually, I'm quite surprised that the police listened to you earlier. They will not do so again, Alba.'

Camille reached out to hug her but Alba shrugged her off. 'I'm not making it up. It's real, I know it!'

When she got to her room, Alba slammed the door hard. For several minutes, she paced up and down clenching and unclenching her fists. It was getting darker now. Alba could see lights going on in the neighbouring houses. She stood by the window. The stone was no longer visible. Alba gave a little sob. Then she remembered the whispered words when she was half asleep. 'Trust yourself, Alba, trust yourself.' Her bag was lying on the floor. Alba felt around inside for the card that the nice policewoman gave to her. WPC Williams had said that Alba could contact her at any time if anything else came to her about Molly.

***

Feeling justified, Alba dialled the number. Lisa Williams picked up immediately. She was on her way home. Another family liaison officer would stay with the Cookson's tonight. Alba told her everything in detail adding, 'Please, you must help, I don't know who else I can ask.' Lisa listened carefully. The girl was in quite a state. She knew that her colleagues would not listen to anything else that Alba told them. Some of them already felt foolish for acting on the child's story earlier. Nevertheless, Lisa could not quite shake the feeling that Alba was seeing what the rest of them failed to see.

Lisa thought of her own mother, who also had an unusual ability to know and see things others could not. Lisa's grandparents used to say their daughter was "fey". Lisa herself was prone to have hunches. Her ambition was to be a detective, so she thought that could be useful. However, she could do nothing official to help Alba at this point. She was off duty, and anyway, she could be risking her career going off on a wild goose chase.

'Are you still there?' Alba asked anxiously. 'Will you help?'

Lisa made up her mind. She would look up the sign name Alba had given her and take it from there. 'Wait a few minutes, Alba. I'm going to check something on my phone,' said Lisa. Alba sat waiting, grateful that something was happening that might help. The phone rang quite quickly. 'Woodland Glade is a holiday resort a few miles away, Alba. It is situated in woodland with several chalets dotted around. It exists. It is real.'

Alba gasped with relief. 'Oh, will the police go there to search for Molly now?'

'I'm afraid not,' replied Lisa. 'They will not search anywhere on the basis of your information. They won't believe you.'

Alba groaned with frustration and was about to reply when the young woman spoke again. 'They won't help but I will, Alba. We'll go together to look for Molly now.'

'But my parents…'

'Don't worry; I shall come to pick you up and speak to them. In the meantime, dress warmly and find a flashlight to bring with you. Give me your address.'

Alba felt giddy with relief. She put together a warm jacket, gumboots and some orange juice and chocolate for Molly. Her friend must be terribly hungry by now. She went downstairs to explain what she was going to do. Her parents were just opening the front door where Lisa Williams stood, showing her badge. Alba hung back while the policewoman carefully explained the plan to her parents. She assured them that Alba would be very safe with her. Camille and David looked at their daughter, who was looking very determined. They both hugged Alba. 'Good luck,' they said quietly.

Lisa and Alba set off. It was dark now. All the houses and streetlamps were lit. Woodland Glade was a bit off the beaten track but Lisa was confident they would find it, despite the dark. She was using her own car but it had first-aid equipment and a blanket already in it.

***

Molly felt very weak. She could not remember how long it had been since she had last had anything to drink or eat. Her ankle still hurt quite a lot but the swelling had not increased. Her jacket was not much protection from the chilly air. Fortunately, there had been no rain. So, at least the hard ground was not wet. Molly had felt too weak to do anything but lie down for several hours now. Her back and hips were sore, and she was very stiff, but all she wanted to do was sleep. She was so very tired.

**

Lisa and Alba saw the sign for Woodland Glade at the same time. Lisa turned off onto the single-track road. Huge trees loomed up in the darkness on both sides of the track. Although the headlights were on full beam, Lisa drove slowly in the dense blackness. The track was leading them upwards now. They climbed for a few minutes, then the track dropped again sharply. Lisa stopped the car and got out to get a better look. The holiday site was probably down below them. She decided to drive down to investigate the accommodation.

They could see a cluster of single-storey holiday chalets down in the glade below. Alba felt a jolt of excitement. The first time she had tried to sense Molly's whereabouts, she had seen something resembling these buildings. All lay in darkness. The chalets appeared to be deserted. Taking both their flashlights, they cautiously began to search the area.

Most of the chalets had curtains in the windows, but they were not drawn. Before shining her flashlight into the interiors, Lisa carefully explored the area around each chalet. Both Alba and Lisa were calling Molly's name but there was nothing. They examined the entire site thoroughly, taking care to look through windows. However, Lisa knew that Molly might be hidden somewhere that the flashlight could not reveal.

By chance, they discovered one chalet that had a key left in the back door. After thoroughly searching it, they discovered that the key opened all the chalet back doors. Painstakingly examining all the interiors, Lisa was sure Molly was not there. The site shop was boarded up, the door padlocked. One small window offered a view of the interior. Lisa shone her light in there but the place seemed empty.

When Lisa and Alba were satisfied they had searched the entire site, they returned to Lisa's car. 'Alba, we have not found anything here. Despite your efforts, I really think we ought to get you back home now. I'm sorry,' said Lisa ruefully.

Alba gulped. 'But I saw the site sign and there were small buildings here as well.'

'I know it's very disappointing, but you tried your best,' said Lisa sympathetically.

Lisa switched on the car engine and lights, preparing to move off. She shook her head sadly;

the girl was clearly upset and needed to be returned home to her parents. Suddenly, Alba grabbed her arm. 'Wait, please wait!' she cried. 'Another picture of Molly has come into my mind. She's here somewhere I know she is.'

Lisa sighed, but turned off the ignition. 'All right then tell me,' she said.

Alba had seen her friend lying next to a very large tree. The picture was just as clear in her mind as the Woodland Glade sign. With the image, a feeling of urgency gripped Alba. She felt that Molly was here and must be found now; there was no more time. Lisa stared. The girl was trembling and still gripping her arm tightly. At this point, the young policewoman decided it was certainly better to be safe than sorry. Even if the rest of the search here proved unproductive, she was not prepared to risk Molly's life. She turned to Alba.

'Let go of my arm,' she said gently, then continued, 'I think there will be lots of trails here in the woods. If Molly is in there somewhere, she might not be too far from the road we drove down. We'll make our way back, stopping frequently to look at where a trail leads off from the road.'

Lisa drove carefully, not expressing her thoughts out loud to Alba, who was looking out of the car window intently. It was dark, the woods looked pretty dense. Goodness knows how many trails led off the road. Even if Molly was in there, the chances of finding her were slim. Lisa tried to put all this out of her mind. A few minutes later, Alba saw a small sign by the side of the road. It was indicating the beginning of the trail walks.

Lisa stopped the car. Taking up her flashlight, first aid, blanket and phone, she set off with Alba. When they reached the small trail sign, they stopped to look in the immediate area, but there was no sign of Molly. Then they had a bit of luck. The clouds were clearing away to reveal the moon shining brightly. Already, they could see more of the densely packed woods. 'Let's walk a little way up this trail, calling Molly's name,' suggested Lisa.

They tried this for a few minutes but no answer came. The trail was leading them upwards; another trail branched out to one side. They decided to keep going upwards, calling Molly's name and stopping to listen. Suddenly, Alba stopped. 'I heard something just then. It seemed to be coming from that direction.' Alba pointed up toward the copse of trees. 'Molly,' she shouted 'are you there'?'

Then they both heard a small cry, that appeared to be coming from the copse. Lisa and Alba practically ran the short distance to where Molly lay. They could see her pale face gazing up at them as they approached. Alba rushed to her friend, who lay sprawled awkwardly on the ground. Molly tried to speak through cracked lips and a very dry mouth, but it turned into a sob.

Lisa dropped down beside her. Trained in first aid, she checked Molly over carefully. The girl was clearly badly dehydrated, and suffering from exposure. Her right ankle was either broken or badly sprained. Lisa swiftly covered Molly with the blanked and motioned Alba to give her just a few mouthfuls of water. As far as Lisa could see, there were no more injuries, but she did not want to leave Molly in case she had missed something. A quick examination of the area around the girl suggested no one else had been there. Lisa quickly called for an ambulance, giving clear precise details of their location in the wood. In the meantime, Alba was kneeling and talking quietly to her friend. Lisa breathed a long sigh of relief, thankful that she had listened to Alba.

Chapter 8
Lives on the Line

Nooka hastened down the small track leading to the boatyard, where her father and Pierre were working. Inatak had run way again. His friend Koyah told her they had been climbing trees, when Inatak suddenly took off. Koyah thought it was because his friend had seen the bad lady going to his house. Concerned, Nooka realised that the social worker must have come to see the family again. She knew that poor little Inatak was due to be put up for adoption soon. *He must be terrified,* she thought. Assuming that Inatak would make for his usual hiding place, Nooka had searched there first, but the child was nowhere to be seen. At this point, Nooka knew she had to have help. Inatak's mother was quite ill at the moment; his father was still away, working. Nooka wanted to find the boy quickly, without worrying his mother. She would ask Pierre for help.

Nooka's father had begun to rely on the young man's help with the boats. Pierre was strong and practical, frequently doing tasks that the older man found difficult. Nooka's father had sustained a serious injury to one of his hands some time ago, that impeded his work. Nevertheless, when Nooka explained the situation and the urgent need of Pierre's help, her father immediately agreed. 'Go, daughter, I shall manage. Run quickly to find the boy,' he said.

Inatak's usual hiding place was near the stream, where Nooka often came. She had bathed the little boy's face and hands after extracting him from the large bush the first time she found him. There was no sign of him having returned there again. Pierre stood looking around.

'A little bit further on, there is a narrow trail leading further into the forest,' he said. 'Do you think the boy would go that far?'

Nooka shook her head at first, but then said, 'He was clearly terrified; he must have thought the social worker had come for him. Maybe in his panic, he did run further.'

Assuming this, the two followed the stream until they reached the trail. Every few yards, they stopped to search either side of the trail, but the bushes there were sparse and thin, not suitable as a hiding place. The trail itself was covered in pine needles and small twigs. Although Pierre knelt down to look carefully for footprints, he could not see any. The forest was alive with sounds. A pair of chirruping chipmunks rushed past them. Jays with their harsh cries fluttered in the trees. They walked on. A bald eagle looked down at them from its perch at the top of a tall Douglas Fir. Another one soared high above in the clear blue sky, its huge wings outspread.

Pierre decided to climb a tree to get a better view of the surrounding area. Choosing a large maple, he climbed quickly and easily. Down below, Nooka gazed up at him, her face pale with anxiety. Not far ahead, Pierre could see a small clearing. He ascended a few more feet to get a better look, and then he froze. Three small black bear cubs were playing in the centre of the clearing. Their mother sat beneath a large grey granite rock, intently watching the top of it. Every now and then her huge mouth opened and she licked the rock. Inatak lay on a narrow ledge, his left leg dangling over the side. Pierre could see the torn trouser-leg and trails of blood on the rock. The child appeared to be conscious, but was very still.

As fast as he could, Pierre climbed down. 'Did you see anything?' asked Nooka.

Pierre nodded, a grim expression on his face. 'Yes, I saw him. He's trapped on a narrow rock ledge.' Nooka gasped. 'But that's not all,' said Pierre. 'There's a bear and three cubs. Mother bear is watching Inatak. She cannot climb the rock to get him, so she's just waiting.'

Nooka put her hand to her mouth, horrified. 'What can we do?' She gulped.

Pierre was silent for a couple of minutes, thinking hard. He put his hand on Nooka's trembling shoulder. 'We have to get the bear away from Inatak somehow,' he said. 'I have an idea how to do that. It's risky, but I can't think of another way. There is no time to go for help. The boy could fall at any minute.'

Nooka nodded in agreement. The child was in imminent danger. They would have to act. But how? 'Bears have such a keen sense of hearing and smell. How could we even get near to him?' she asked nervously.

Pierre explained his plan. To attract Inatak's attention, but not the bear's, he would use his metal belt-buckle to reflect the sun. Hopefully, he could train the light onto the boy's face to alert him. Pierre would be visible, but silent, up another tree. Ideally, he would be upwind of the bear. However, this was not possible. When he knew that the boy had seen him, Pierre would join Nooka at ground level. They would silently get as close to the clearing as possible.

Nooka listened, then asked, 'Even if she does not hear us coming, surely, she'll smell us?'

Pierre nodded. 'This is why everything will happen very fast. The whole plan is dangerous, I know, Nooka, but it's the only one we've got.'

Nooka listened intently and with growing trepidation, as Pierre told her the rest of his plan.

When they got to the clearing, Pierre would dash towards the nearest cub, as if to pick it up. Then he would run away as fast as he could, hoping mother bear would come after him. Immediately, Nooka would go to get Inatak and run back towards the village.

Nooka clung to Pierre. She was terrified that the bear would catch and kill him. Bears could run very fast. Pierre held the quivering girl close. 'I was a champion runner at school, Nooka. I can do this,' he assured her. 'You concentrate on Inatak.' He was feeling far from sure that he could outrun the bear, but he did not want to alarm Nooka any further.

Pierre chose another large maple nearer the clearing. Silently, he climbed to a point where he could make a signal. Holding on tightly with his right hand, he stretched out his left hand, holding the belt buckle. This quickly caught the sun, enabling him to shine its reflection onto Inatak's face. The little boy still had not moved, but after the light flickered a few times, he opened his eyes. Squinting, he looked up, following the moving light. His eyes widened when he saw Pierre, who had put his finger to his lips, motioning him to keep silent.

Down on the ground now, Pierre led Nooka silently to a clump of bushes, where both could see into the clearing. Nooka stopped herself putting her hand to her mouth when she saw Inatak. Instead, she readied herself for Pierre's signal. The three cubs were still at play, their mother focused on the boy. Pierre clenched then unclenched his fists. Then taking a deep breath, he hurtled into the clearing, towards one of the cubs, reaching his arms out to it. Then, swerving abruptly, he raced away. The bear bellowed with rage and charged after him.

Nooka then dashed forward. The little boy looked at her with terrified eyes. Swiftly, Nooka took in the state of him, particularly his wounded leg dangling over the edge of the rock. Reaching up her arms, she cried, 'Inatak, roll off! I'll catch you!' The child was rigid with fear, unable to move. 'Now! Now!' screamed Nooka. 'We haven't got much time. Come on!' Inatak fell heavily into Nooka's outstretched arms. She fell back; Inatak sprawled on top of her.

'Climb on my back,' Nooka gasped. She was winded badly and struggled to get her breath. The boy managed to clamber onto her back, putting his little arms around her neck. Nooka grabbed his legs, holding him tightly around his waist.

Heaving them both up, Nooka ran, Inatak hanging on as they charged out of the clearing. On the trail, Nooka did not try to look back. Even when they reached the path to the village, she did not slacken her pace. Finally, panting hard, she ran into the village, where people quickly came to help.

Trying to get her breath, she managed a feeble smile as two of the villagers lifted Inatak from her. Then she fell back, exhausted. Inatak was swiftly taken by the women to deal with his wound.

Nooka was desperately worried about Pierre. There was no sign of him yet. She prayed he got away safely. The whole rescue could have taken minutes or even an hour. She had lost track of time.

Suddenly, one of the men shouted and pointed as Pierre emerged from the trees, limping his way towards the path. One man on each side supporting Pierre, they helped him into the village. Pierre's face was scratched and bloody, his clothes were torn, and he was drenched in sweat. Gently, they half-carried him to where Nooka sat on the ground. Someone fetched a blanket and some water. Nooka cradled Pierre's head in her lap.

'Oh, I'm so glad you're safe. I was so afraid for you.' Pierre managed a slight smile. Nooka placed a pillow under his head and left him to rest.

A couple of hours later, he was well enough to tell his part in the rescue. Nooka had already told hers. Little Inatak was recovering from the ordeal. He was at the local nurses' station, having the gash on his leg sewn up and being treated for shock.

Pierre recounted how, when he raced off from the clearing, the bear charged after him, her cubs trailing after her. Pierre ran faster than he had ever run in his life. Swerving and twisting around bushes and trees, he tried to shake off the bear, but she kept coming. The bear was gaining on him. He felt her hot breath on his back. With a desperate final push, he forced himself on, knowing the bear would show him no mercy if she caught him. Suddenly, he could no longer hear her lumbering behind him. Still, he kept on running, until he felt safe enough to turn and look back. He saw the bear together with her three cubs. She had given up the chase.

***

Alba rose very early on the Monday, despite having had little sleep the night before. She very much wanted to thank the Lady of the Flowers for her help. Without this, her best friend might not have been found in time to save her life. Molly was now being cared for in hospital. Fortunately, being young and fit, she was recovering from her ordeal very well. Her ankle was badly sprained but it would heal. Her parents were with her now, but the police were waiting a few hours before talking to her.

WPC Lisa Williams had already given her colleagues a detailed report of the circumstances that led to Molly's discovery. She need not have worried that she would receive a reprimand for her unorthodox behaviour. In fact, her boss congratulated her on her ingenuity and quick-thinking; all good qualities for a budding detective. Lisa also spoke very highly of Alba, describing her as a girl of exceptional ability. She particularly commended Alba for her refusal to give up on her friend, despite people failing to believe her. For Lisa herself, it had been a valuable learning experience. In future police investigations, she would remember that leads can come from very unexpected quarters.

The grass was laden with dew, the sun just coming through the clouds, as Alba reached the stone seat. She found herself greeting the birds and flowers as if they were old friends. Alba smiled, realising that she liked that part of herself. Being in nature worked for her. She had always found solace there in difficult times. Now, this morning, she felt both happiness and gratitude.

As these feelings rose up within her, she saw the shimmering outline of the lady. 'Greetings, dear Alba. Is it not a beautiful morning?' she said with a warm smile. 'I think that you have found much since we last talked.'

'Oh yes,' replied Alba eagerly. 'I found that when I was able to trust my odd feelings—my intuition, I mean—it was much better.'

'So, you found Molly, and you found your true self,' said the lady.

Alba nodded thoughtfully. 'I think I understand myself a bit more now, but I couldn't have done it without you.'

'Dear Alba,' replied the lady gently, 'I was merely helping you to access your own inner wisdom; for you to discover who you really are, and who you might become.'

Alba sat quietly absorbing the lady's words. She felt that she had a gentle teacher, who was encouraging her to believe in herself. Alba was finding all this very helpful. She closed her eyes, aware of the sun warm on her face, and of a warm feeling inside her, as if she herself had an inner bright sun. 'Thank you,' she whispered gratefully.

Alba was surprised by the number of children who quickly surrounded her when she arrived at school. Word of Molly's rescue had spread quickly. Even girls who had not been particularly pleasant to Alba clustered around her, asking questions eagerly. At morning assembly, the headmaster asked her to come out to the front, where he praised her part in the rescue. Alba blushed deep red when he described her as a heroine. She didn't feel like one. Still, it was rather thrilling when the entire school applauded her. As she walked back to her place, she speculated whether she would get applause like that when she performed in the forthcoming play.

Lessons went smoothly. Several of her teachers made a point of congratulating her. Both break and lunchtime saw Alba in the middle of groups, all jostling for her story. At the end of the school day, Alba was feeling pretty tired. The events of the weekend, and the loss of last night's sleep, were taking their toll.

When she arrived home, her mother had some news. Molly's parents had called to say they had found Molly's phone. Apparently, it was on the floor underneath a heavy armchair. They only discovered it when they went to get a small suitcase from the hall cupboard. They were taking some clothes to the hospital for Molly. The heavy chair was next to the cupboard, and had not been moved for ages. They were able to see many of the messages "Tim" had sent their daughter, as well as his picture. They gave the phone to WPC Williams, who was able to restore 'Tim's' deleted texts. Those final messages described in detail the time and place of his proposed meeting with Molly. This further information was very helpful to the police.

With Molly's description of the man she saw lurking around the chalet, they were able to identify a suspect. This was someone who had been regularly posing as a teenage boy on social media. He had a very unsavoury background. Molly was a very lucky girl, the police told her parents. Mr and Mrs Cookson were just grateful to have their daughter back safely. Molly was very contrite. She promised faithfully she'd never involve herself in anything like that again.

Alba slept soundly for a good ten hours that night. On her way to bed, Camille looked in on her daughter sleeping peacefully. She regretted that she and her husband had not believed Alba. Camille was also ashamed that her daughter felt forced to ask for help from the young policewoman. Alba was brave and resourceful, Camille realised. She also recognised that her dreamy and sensitive daughter had a special gift. Nooka was like that. Camille remembered her mother always had a way of knowing what was troubling her daughter, without being told. She too could find lost things, and sensed coming events before they happened. Camille gazed at her sleeping daughter.

'*How she must miss Nooka. They were always so close,*' she remembered sadly. As she quietly closed Alba's door, Camille resolved to be there for her daughter more fully, now that she had a better understanding of Alba's nature.

***

Nooka sat with Pierre on the bank of the stream. It had become their favourite place to meet. Pierre had completely recovered from his encounter with the bear. Inatak was back home with his mother.

His leg was still rather sore and he limped a little. The main problem was the nightmares. Every night, he woke screaming with fear from being chased by a large monster. Each time, he woke just as the monster opened its huge mouth, about to devour him. Inatak was afraid to leave the house and go out to play. When his mother went to their outside yard, he clung to her skirts. He spent most of the time looking out of the window, anticipating with dread the reappearance of the bad lady. His mother constantly suffered with her health problems, made worse with the constant worrying about her youngest child. Her husband was not due home for a few more weeks. She longed for his support now more than ever. Had Tahoma not been taken from her, she would have had his help. She wept daily for the loss of her beloved older son. He would never come back to them.

Nooka had finally been released from the dreadful school. Now, at nearly sixteen, attendance was no longer compulsory. She delighted in being back with her parents and threw herself into helping out in the village wherever she could. Most mornings, she went into the small village school where the youngest children were. Those under seven were allowed by the authorities to stay at home.

Nooka spent many happy mornings with the children, assisting the native teachers. She loved telling them stories of their culture and singing the old songs with them. Nooka hoped that these experiences would help sustain them when they got sent away to the residential schools.

Pierre spent most of his time working with Nooka's father. He had become a skilful fisherman under her father's tutelage. Many of the villagers had come to like and respect the young French Canadian. However, others were still suspicious of this white man. They had no reason to trust white people, who created so many problems for them.

These views were expressed to Nooka's father in a meeting of the band council. Listening carefully to their concerns, he acknowledged that in general, white people had made their lives very difficult in many ways. However, he explained that in his view, an alliance with this particular white man could be a good thing. He was aware of the increasingly close relationship between Pierre and Nooka. He trusted the young man's intentions towards his only daughter. Quite apart from rescuing Inatak, Pierre seemed genuinely to care about First Nations people and their lives. He was willing to approach the Department of Indian Affairs to prevent Inatak from being taken from his family.

Chapter 9
A Village Wedding

Lucy Jenkins returned to her classroom after a conversation with the headmaster. He had called her in to discuss a delicate matter concerning Evie Harris aged twelve. There were already concerns about the girl's increasingly disturbed behaviour over the past few weeks. However, the situation concerning the Harris family had worsened. Social workers had been trying very hard to help the family, who were in serious difficulty. It now appeared that Evie and her siblings were likely to be placed in care separately. The social workers had tried everything they could to keep the children together, but to no avail. The headmaster wanted all his staff who taught Evie to be aware of the situation, so that they could support the child as much as possible in these distressing circumstances.

Lucy sighed deeply; this was a sad moment for Evie and her family. Lucy had tried to encourage Evie to talk to her about her increasingly bad behaviour, but Evie was uncommunicative. She sat silent and sullen, often glaring at Lucy through red-rimmed eyes. Evie was a bright girl who, until the past few months, was a joy to teach. She was no longer an outgoing, happy girl. Now, she could be withdrawn or behave disruptively. Even her friends took to sitting further away from her in class.

Lucy thought hard about what she could do to help the girl. Evie's year were performing '*Lost at Sea*' very soon. Although the play had been cast, there were other backstage positions to fill. Perhaps she could tempt Evie to take charge of props. This was an important part of the production, and Evie might enjoy making sure that all the characters had their various props efficiently provided. This could be cups and saucers, brush and comb, letters and papers. Perhaps being in charge of something at school might help, when everything else in her life was such a mess. Lucy thought this was a reasonable plan.

The play rehearsals were going extremely well. Lucy was particularly pleased with the way Alba was handling her role as Harriet, the oldest child. She obviously loved to act, and had considerable talent. Not many weeks ago Alba was often sad and rather withdrawn. The loss of her grandmother had affected her deeply. Now she was more her old self and in addition, she seemed to have matured. Always a kind, caring girl, there was something extra now, a special quality that Lucy had not seen before. She found herself wondering how this had come about. Smiling to herself, she thought, '*Well, whatever it is, it's certainly working well for Alba.*'

Alba packed up a few goodies for Molly and cycled off to see her friend. She had not seen Molly since the night of the rescue. But the two had chatted regularly on their phones. Things had settled down for the Cookson's, much to everyone's relief. Molly's mother greeted Alba with a smile and a big hug. 'She's in the sitting room.'

The two friends were soon deep in conversation. Molly was keen to know all the latest school news. Though her ankle was healing well, she needed a bit more recovery time before resuming school. Being at home was beginning to bore her, so she wanted to know every detail.

Alba was eager to talk about the forthcoming play and how well it was all going. As well as her fellow members of the cast of *Lost at Sea*, Alba knew about other children in the same year who had been chosen to be involved backstage. Molly frowned. 'Did you say Evie Harris would be backstage?'

'What?' said Alba. 'Oh yes, Miss Jenkins has asked her to be in charge of props.'

Molly nodded thoughtfully. 'It's just that Evie is part of the group who were mean to you. You remember when you got the part, they said that you were too dark to play the role of Harriet?' Molly bit her lip. 'I heard Evie saying it more than once. She really doesn't like you, Alba.'

Alba laughed and said breezily, 'Miss Jenkins said that it didn't matter. She explained that, even though the play described the fisherman father as a Dutchman with fair hair and blue eyes, and children of a similar colouring, it wasn't important. Miss Jenkins told us she was pleased to do colour-blind casting.'

Molly looked puzzled. 'How do you mean?'

Alba carefully explained how Miss Jenkins told them she had selected the cast on the basis of their acting ability and that their colouring was not important.

Both girls agreed that their teacher was right. They liked the fact that Miss Jenkins treated everyone the same, and was always fair. Like most children, they were keenly observant and easily able to spot the teachers who were not genuine.

Molly hesitated, then said, 'Er… I know Miss Jenkins is really busy with the play, but she still hasn't marked my essay. I really worked hard on it, and handed it in a long time ago. It took me ages to write it.' Molly could see that Alba was only half-listening, so she sighed and added, 'I'm really looking forward to seeing the play. My parents are as well.'

The girls chatted for a couple of hours then Alba left to cycle home.

***

David and Camille were relaxing over a cup of tea in the garden. Unusually, David had an afternoon off, and had been helping his wife do some weeding. It was a welcome break from his stressful work. Sipping his tea, he decided he would update Camille concerning a difficult case he was involved in. Alba might inadvertently be affected, so he felt he needed to put Camille in the picture.

For some time, he had been trying to prevent the Harris family from being split up. Now, however, it appeared inevitable that all three children would be placed in care separately. As the senior social worker, David was in overall charge of the case, but his fieldworker had been dealing directly with the family. Like David, his colleague had tried extremely hard to keep the family together.

The oldest child, Evie Harris, attended the same school as Alba, and was in the same year. Obviously, Alba knew nothing of all this. The headmaster and staff were fully informed and were being very supportive. However, David's fieldworker had expressed considerable concern for Evie. The poor girl was distraught. Her teachers were very concerned by her increasingly disturbed behaviour. Her peers at school were turning away from her. David's fieldworker was conscientious and professional in his dealings with the Harris family. However, David could not entirely shrug off the worry that it might accidentally leak out that Evie Harris and Alba were in the same year at school. It was unlikely, but nevertheless, in delicate situations like this it was a worry.

Camille thought her husband looked strained as he drank his tea. She touched his arm gently. 'Can you talk about it, David? I know how confidential your work is, but I'm concerned something is really bothering you.' David sighed, then began to carefully explain his concerns regarding the situation.

***

Nooka smiled to herself as she brushed her long dark hair. Outside, she could hear the excited chatter of the villagers, as they prepared for the wedding celebrations. Pierre had suggested they have a civil registry office ceremony in the nearby town, followed by a traditional celebration in the village.

Pierre loved his work as a fisherman. He had been taught well by Nooka's father, who greatly valued the young French Canadian. Pierre felt very at home in the village. He made a point of taking an interest in the village life, making contributions whenever he could.

Nooka laid down her hairbrush and looked out of the window. A small group of children were playing on ropes dangling from some trees. In the middle was Inatak, laughing and chatting excitedly, his little face beaming with happiness. Nooka smiled broadly as she watched him behaving like the carefree small boy he now was.

After consultation with the village elders, Pierre had gone to meet with the social worker at the Department for Indian Affairs. He explained carefully and in detail how he intended to help Inatak's family over the coming months. He gave assurances that he would not only keep an eye on Inatak, but he would help to support the family financially. Inatak's father was still having to work long periods away from home, and money was tight. He told the social worker that Nooka, his future wife, would also help the family. She too would keep a special eye on Inatak, and in addition would help Inatak's mother to cope with her household tasks.

At first, the social worker resisted this plan, saying that arrangements had already been made for Inatak's adoption and she could not change them. However, after several visits from Pierre, she realised that the young man was quite determined and would not drop the matter. Eventually, she gave in. The whole village celebrated that little Inatak was safe.

Nooka walked over to the children's play area. Inatak immediately ran to her, throwing his arms around her waist. Laughing, Nooka took his hand. 'Shall we go to our special place?' she said.

Together, they set off towards the forest, making for the little stream they often visited together. Inatak ran ahead, and with a delighted chuckle, jumped into the shallow water. Watching the little boy splashing merrily in the clear water, Nooka thought back to the day when Inatak might have died. She still shuddered when she recalled the bear licking Inatak's blood off the rock. His leg had healed well, with only a faint scar where the bear had clawed him. Nooka still felt amazed that Pierre had been able to outrun the bear. Not only that, she would not have believed that she was strong enough to run so fast, carrying a child on her back. She thought to herself how resourceful human beings could be when they were faced with great danger. It would be an experience that Nooka was to remember all of her life.

A damp little hand nudged her out of her reverie. 'These are for you, Nooka,' said Inatak, as he carefully placed a number of small, brightly coloured stones in her lap. 'I can make them into a bracelet for you to wear at your wedding,' said the little boy gazing at her, his huge brown eyes lit with joy.

'They are beautiful, Inatak,' said Nooka softly.

Pierre was waiting at her parents' house when they returned. He was dressed and all ready for their wedding celebrations early that evening. Inatak smiled up at the tall young man, showing him the pretty stones. The two wandered off to make Nooka the bracelet. Her mother was beckoning her to get dressed for the wedding.

Nooka's mother helped her to put on her wedding dress, which was full-skirted, and made from brightly coloured material. She braided her daughter's hair, carefully arranging it in elaborate coils around Nooka's head. Then she placed wild flowers of delicate colours in between the braids. Nooka and Pierre were sorry that his parents were too infirm to make the journey from Montreal. However, they had sent gifts for Nooka's parents, and money for the young couple.

Sounds of excited chatter and laughter came from the centre of the village. All the villagers were gathering for the ceremony, everyone dressed in bright colours. Some carried drums, some tambourines. All the children held posies of wild flowers. There would be feasting on roast turkey and homemade cakes. This was also a joyous opportunity for everyone to sing old and new songs. All would take part in the dancing, except for the drummers. On this special occasion, little Inatak had permission from the elders to play his drum, a present from Pierre.

Nooka's father knocked gently on the door. 'We are ready now, beloved daughter,' said her father, smiling proudly. 'I will walk with you.'

Nooka could see Pierre waiting for her in the centre of the gathering. Beaming smiles surrounded the couple, who stood quietly holding hands. Grinning broadly, Inatak began to beat his little drum.

And then the fun began. After much feasting, singing and dancing, the villagers settled down for the potlatch. In the ceremony, Nooka's parents distributed small gifts to all the village families. Festivities went on for many hours. Nooka leaned her head on Pierre's shoulder.

'Could we slip away for just a few minutes to our special place?'

'Why not?' murmured Pierre. 'The moon is full, the sky cloudless. We can easily find our way.' And so, they walked hand in hand toward the forest and their new life together.

**

Alba drew aside her bedroom curtains. The morning was bright, the summer flowers scenting the air. Looking across to the stone seat, Alba noticed that white and red roses were in full bloom around it. She wanted to be with the lady this morning. In just a few days, it would be the first night of the school play, '*Lost at Sea*'. Alba had mixed feelings. She was looking forward so much to the performance, and yet she was scared. Would she remember her lines? There were a lot. Would she be convincing as Harriet, the lead character? Alba's tummy rumbled with the familiar butterflies. Sighing, she walked slowly towards the stone seat.

Next door's cat ran across the grass towards her, mewing happily as Alba bent to stroke her gently. The little cat gazed up at her, its golden eyes shining bright in the morning sun. Seeing a butterfly, it scampered off to give chase.

Alba sat on the warm stone and closed her eyes. She felt a very light touch on her arm. Glancing down, she saw a beautiful red admiral butterfly perched on her wrist, its wings spread and quivering slightly. Alba became very still, lest she disturb the little creature. She gazed at the butterfly, at its delicate proboscis and bright colours. She thought to herself that a butterfly is like a flying flower. Several minutes passed. The butterfly seemed happy to be resting on her arm. Alba began to feel very relaxed and peaceful. She smiled faintly as she realised the butterflies in her tummy were no longer there. A soft rose-scented breeze lifted the butterfly's wings, and it flew off.

Alba saw her; the Lady of the Flowers shimmering and smiling gently. 'Greetings, Alba. I see you were admiring the beautiful butterfly just now.'

Alba looked at the lady gratefully. 'Yes, I was, I'm so glad you are here again.'

The lady nodded. 'And what did you see and feel when you looked at the butterfly?'

Alba replied slowly and deliberately. 'Well, I was pleased when it landed on my arm. It was so delicate, its colour and wings made me think it's like a flying flower. I was also amazed that those delicate wings could withstand being blown by wind and rain,' she added.

'That is very perceptive of you, Alba,' said the lady. She went on, 'Do you know what transformation means?'

Alba thought. 'Er… not really, no.'

'Let us consider both the butterfly and the flower, Alba, and how they come into being. The butterfly begins as a small grub, then it changes into a chrysalis, then into a butterfly, yes?'

'Yes,' replied Alba. 'I learned that at school.'

'Good,' said the lady. 'Now the flower. How does this begin?'

Alba replied eagerly, 'It begins as a seed in the ground, then it becomes a shoot and finally it blooms as a flower.'

'Indeed,' said the lady. 'This is called transformation. A state of becoming, you see.'

Alba smiled. 'Yes, I understand now. Grub transforms into a butterfly, seed transforms into a flower.'

The lady smiled and continued. 'You, dear Alba, like the butterfly and the flower, are also transforming.'

Alba gazed at the lady. 'Am I?' she asked wonderingly.

'Yes, indeed, Alba, you are also changing as you grow. You too are in a state of becoming—— becoming who you truly are. All the experiences you have help you to learn and to grow.'

Alba thought about this carefully. 'But I'm scared now about the school play. I don't like the experience of being scared. Perhaps you mean that we grow only through good experiences,' she said, feeling rather puzzled.

The lady laughed softly. 'Ah, Alba, you learn and grow through all experiences, good and bad. This may seem strange to you now, but I believe that you may come to understand this a little more soon.'

Alba sat listening carefully to the lady's words, wondering if or how she would come to understand their meaning. 'Thank you,' she said quietly.

'Before we finish our conversation today,' the lady added, 'I wish to say something further. Trust in yourself, Alba. You know more than you think you know. Be assured of this, child.'

A single white rose petal fell into Alba's open hand. Silence. The lady had gone.

Chapter 10
Sabotage and Success

Lucy Jenkins was very pleased with everyone involved in '*Lost at Sea*'. The children were working hard, and enjoying themselves. Lucy made sure that the backstage group felt as valued as the actors. She stressed the importance of everyone working hard as a team, to make sure the play went well.

'*Lost at Sea*' was set in a small English fishing village at the beginning of the 20th century. A Dutch fisherman, his wife and three children lived in a cottage. Harriet, the oldest child, shared the responsibility for caring for the little family with her mother, when their father was away fishing. In the small fishing community, friends and neighbours helped out as much as they could.

When the father was thought drowned after a shipwreck, the family struggled to get by. However, all ended happily when a letter arrived from the father, saying he had survived.

The children with acting roles had fun dressing up in old-fashioned clothes. Alba was playing the lead role of Harriet, who was a couple of years older than Alba. Miss Jenkins showed Alba how to put her hair up to make her look older. It helped that Alba was tall for her age.

The day before the first night of the play, Camille called Alba downstairs. Her daughter was still studying her lines, even though she was word-perfect in rehearsal.

Camille smiled. 'Alba, I have just come across something precious that Nooka gave me when I was a little girl. I thought it was lost forever, but it had just fallen into a gap at the back of my dressing table drawer.'

Alba saw a small bracelet made from tiny, bright-coloured stones, woven together with small strips of leather.

'Oh, that's so pretty!' said Alba delightedly. 'I love the bright colours.'

'This bracelet is very special,' said Camille. 'Before they were married, Nooka and your grandfather, Pierre, rescued a little boy from a bear. It was very dangerous doing this, but they managed. My father was a very fast runner. He led the bear away from the little boy so that Nooka could run to rescue the child. The bear had cubs, so it was especially dangerous.'

Alba was thrilled to hear this. Her grandmother had always been modest, never boasting about anything. 'But what has the bracelet got to do with it?' asked Alba.

'Well,' said Camille 'just before Nooka and Pierre's wedding, the little boy collected the stones as a wedding present for them. He and Pierre fashioned the stones into a bracelet.'

Smiling, Alba said, 'What a lovely story. I'm so glad you've found it now.'

Camille took Alba's hand and gently laid the bracelet in it. 'I want you to have it now. I think Nooka would want that too.' Both mother and daughter had tears in their eyes as they remembered a beloved mother and grandmother.

Alba hugged Camille tightly. 'I love it, Mum. Thank you. I'm always thinking about Nooka. I miss her so much. When I hold her bracelet, I feel close to her again.'

Alba decided to cycle over to see Molly. It was early evening, the sun still high in the sky. She was longing to show her friend Nooka's bracelet. When she arrived, Molly was sitting in the garden reading. She waved happily to Alba, who quickly parked her bike and ran down to join her. 'Look, Mum has just given this to me,' said Alba.

Molly held the bracelet up so that the sun shone on the brightly coloured stones. 'It's so beautiful,' she murmured. 'I haven't seen anything like this before.'

Alba eagerly told Molly the intriguing story of Nooka's bracelet. 'I'm going to wear it in the play.

My costume has long sleeves so it won't show,' she added.

The girls chatted happily until Mrs Cookson called from the kitchen window. 'It's getting a bit late, Alba, and you need a good night's sleep before the play starts its run. We'll all see you tomorrow night.'

With the bracelet safely in her pocket, Alba rode home.

The next day, the cast and backstage crew were buzzing with excitement. Even Lucy Jenkins had arrived very early to check everything was in its place, both onstage and backstage. Lucy checked that the fishing net was in place in the props room. Harriet mended nets to bring money in for the poor family. Her character also played the piano sometimes for a rich lady, who lived outside the village. The school production could not stage this, of course, but Harriet talked about it to her mother.

Lucy carefully checked that the letter was in place. This was extremely important, because it would arrive at the end of the play. The letter would reveal that the father was alive and well. He had managed to survive the shipwreck and was on his way home. This was the climax of the play, and an opportunity for Alba, as Harriet, to really demonstrate her acting skills, as she read her father's letter. Half-laughing, half-tearful, she would read the letter to her younger siblings. It was a very emotional moment and a happy ending to the play.

The headmaster was allowing all the children involved in the play special permission to leave early for the next few days. Lucy Jenkins took a final look around the stage set. Satisfied, she went to the staffroom to do a large pile of marking. This had rather built up over the past weeks, due to her extra work on the play. Lucy sank gratefully into an old armchair, a mug of coffee in one hand, her marking pen in the other.

***

Evie Harris came out of the girls' toilet. She had been released from Mr Bolt's lesson so she could go home early, like the others in the play. She looked around her; no one else was in the corridor. Evie did not want to go home. In fact, she dreaded going home. In a few days, she would be taken to a foster home and separated from her family.

The social worker had tried to be kind. He explained that he had done all he could to prevent Evie and her siblings from being split up. He said he hoped it would be a temporary measure, but was not able to tell her how long she would be fostered. Evie had sobbed so hard she could not get her breath. Her tears mixed with snot from her nose ran down her t-shirt.

'No!' she had gasped. 'No, I won't go, you can't make me!'

The social worker looked at her, feeling miserable himself. He loved his work, but these situations were very upsetting. He reached out his hand, but Evie batted it away and rushed out of the room.

Evie walked along the corridor quietly. She needed to find somewhere to be on her own until the time came for the play to begin that evening. Miss Jenkins had persuaded her to be in charge of the props. First, she had refused, but Miss Jenkins had said that Evie would be very good, and she needed someone who could be responsible for this important task. Evie smiled faintly. Miss Jenkins had been really nice to her, despite everything.

Evie knew she had been really badly behaved with everyone. Part of her felt ashamed, but the other part felt so very angry and hurt. She was lashing out at a world that was cruel and unfair. Miss Jenkins had gone out of her way to be helpful, but Evie had not been able to open up to her. Sometimes, she felt so angry she thought she would explode into tiny pieces.

'Then they'll be sorry,' she muttered to herself.

Evie found she was walking to the small room at the back of the stage, where all the props were. Silently, she entered the room, which was very dark. Rather than switch on the light, Evie sat disconsolately on the floor. Her stomach rumbled. She had eaten nothing much all day. Her job that evening was to make sure that the actors got the props they needed onstage. Evie looked at the fishing net, in a heap in the corner. This was for Alba to mend. Evie bit her lip. Harriet was the lead role in the play and Alba had been chosen for it.

'She would, of course, wouldn't she, miss goody-goody!' she muttered. 'Oh yes, she'll be a star.'

Evie felt the anger building inside her so much she felt sick. It was all so unfair. Why should Alba have a nice life while hers was in ruins? Her heart thumping, Evie muttered every swearword she had ever heard. Then she sat up straight. She suddenly knew what she was going to do. Crossing to the table where the small props were carefully placed, Evie reached for the letter. The climax of the play was Harriet receiving the letter from her father. It was the most dramatic part of the whole play. Alba would open the envelope, take out the letter, then read it to her mother and siblings. Evie knew that the letter was quite long and that Alba would probably not have learned the words. After all, why should she, when all she had to do was read the words on the page?

Carefully, Evie removed the letter from its envelope and substituted a plain piece of paper. She sealed the envelope, putting the real letter in her pocket. A nasty smile widened on her face, as Evie contemplated Alba's shock when she opened the letter.

At six, everyone arrived to get ready. The children were tremendously excited, looking forward to the performance. Their parents and other relatives would be in the audience, as well as school friends. There were to be three performances altogether, and tickets had been sold for all three nights. The local newspaper was sending a reporter tonight to review the play. It was the first time *'Lost at Sea'* was being performed by a school.

Alba and the other children put on their costumes. Lucy Jenkins and several members of staff helped them. Wearing stage makeup was great fun. All the cast looked very convincing with different hairstyles and period costumes. Nooka's bracelet was on Alba's left wrist, hidden underneath the long sleeve of her blouse. She touched it with her right hand. 'I wish you could have been here tonight, Nooka,' she said under her breath.

Lucy Jenkins, looking flushed and happy, came over to her. 'All set, Alba?' she asked with a smile. 'In the theatre, actors say "break a leg" to other actors to wish them luck,' she added.

Alba laughed. 'That's a funny thing to say, miss.'

Lucy smiled again and went off to fix someone's makeup.

The school hall was filling up, friends and parents finding their seats, greeting those they knew. Molly Cookson and her parents were there, as were Alfie and his family. They smiled and waved to David and Camille as they made their way to their seats. After everyone had filed in and found their seats, the headmaster walked to the front of the stage. He welcomed everyone warmly, saying the play would be in two acts and that there would be an interval between. Biscuits, juice, coffee and tea would be served in the interval.

The first act went swimmingly. All the children remembered their lines and there were no glitches. Alba was amazed how quickly the time passed. Miss Jenkins had an encouraging word for everyone during the interval. She was delighted. The audience seemed to be enjoying it. They were listening intently and clapped enthusiastically at the end of the first act. Lucy carefully checked the stage and the props to make sure everything was in its place for the second and final act. That done, she found a quiet corner and sipped coffee from her flask.

The second act opened well, the cast even more confident. All the actors were at their very best, and clearly enjoying the opportunity to perform such an interesting play.

Ten minutes from the end...

Harriet has just finished telling her younger brother and sister a story, when the postman knocks on the door. Smart in his uniform, he stands there touching his hat respectfully, as he addresses Harriet.

'Miss, I have a letter for the family. I was told it is very important because it has come all the way from Holland.' Solemnly, he hands the letter to Harriet, who is looking at him with startled, wide-open eyes.

Putting her hand to her throat, she replies in a shaky voice, 'Er... thank you. Thank you very much.'

The postman smiles, tips his hat again, then leaves.

Harriet's brother and sister look at her open-mouthed. 'What is it, Harriet?' asks her little brother.

'Harriet shakes her head. 'I am not sure, Jamie, but I must take it to Mother straight away.' Holding the younger ones' hands, Harriet goes into her mother's room. Their mother is sleeping, so the children gather round. Harriet touches her mother gently on the shoulder. 'Mother, we have a letter from Holland!'

Mother gives a little gasp. 'Please open it, dear.'

Harriet's hands tremble as she opens the envelope. Watching from the wings, Lucy Jenkins is again impressed with Alba's acting. The audience is absolutely silent, waiting with anticipation. Harriet slowly draws the folded letter out of the envelope and carefully unfolds it.

Alba begins to tremble properly now. She's not pretending. With shock, she sees only a blank sheet of paper. There are no words to read. She stares blankly at the paper. The audience is tense and hushed. She never learned the words of the long letter. She never needed to.

Alba takes a quick glance at Jamie and his sister. Both children look at her with puzzled expressions. In rehearsal, Alba, as Harriet, had quickly begun to read the letter in a very excited voice. Now Harriet is silent. Even Harriet's mother whispers 'Alba?' while hiding her mouth with her hand.

Lucy Jenkins stares hard at Alba. *'What's the matter with the girl? This dramatic pause has gone on too long,'* she thinks anxiously.

Some of the audience are shifting in their chairs, some whispering. Camille, David and Molly, watching Alba, sense something is wrong.

But what? Camille can see that even with her stage makeup, her daughter has become extremely pale.

'Oh heavens!' says Lucy to herself, 'I have to prompt her.'

In these seconds of being silent, Alba's head spins. She has to do something or the play will be ruined. Strangely, the Lady of the Flowers seems to speak in her mind. 'Trust yourself, Alba. You know more than you think you know.' Alba holds Nooka's bracelet tightly for a brief moment. Then she takes a deep breath.

Holding the letter firmly in front of her, she reads it. She speaks clearly as Harriet, reading every word of her father's letter to the family. She describes in detail the Dutch fisherman's shipwreck. How he was rescued off the coast of Holland. How he was taken, seriously injured, to hospital, where he lay in a coma. He could not give his name and address in England, so the hospital was unable to notify his family. Harriet's father describes at length all the time it took for his recovery. Finally, after many weeks, he was able to write to the family, and prepare to travel home. He found a place on a fishing boat returning to England. Hopefully, not long after receiving his letter, the family would be seeing him again.

Alba takes a deep shuddering breath of relief.

The End.

The audience just erupted. The applause was deafening, as one by one they got to their feet. David, Camille and Molly stood clapping and cheering. In the wings, Lucy Jenkins was also clapping loudly.

'Wow! What a performance, Alba!' she said to herself.

At this moment, no one knew that Alba had not had a letter to read, except for one person, of course. She had now crept quietly away.

The entire cast took many bows, with Alba in the middle. Then Lucy Jenkins came out with her backstage crew. All were roundly applauded. Alba smiled until her cheeks ached. She saw her parents, Molly and Alfie all standing, clapping and cheering. First thing tomorrow she would go to the stone seat. She could not wait to be with the Lady of the Flowers. There was so much to tell her.

Alba tossed and turned in bed that night. She was much too excited to sleep. She was reliving the whole play in her mind. Vividly, she recalled the awful shock when she opened the letter. This was the dramatic climax of the entire play. Alba shuddered when she remembered being faced with a blank sheet of paper. Time seemed to stand still in that moment, her mind as blank as the paper. And yet, in that awful pause, something amazing had happened. Although she had never learned the words of the letter, they just seemed to appear in her mind. She found herself speaking them clearly.

Alba was to later learn that this was called "ad libbing". Actors would sometimes have to make up words very quickly in a performance, if something went wrong. For someone like Alba, with little experience acting on stage, what she achieved was extraordinary.

After the performance, Miss Jenkins told Alba she had discovered the real letter later, crumpled on the floor backstage. She described how the long dramatic pause Alba took, before reading the letter, concerned her at the time. However, on learning that Alba was faced with a blank sheet of paper, she was shocked and amazed. Smiling broadly, Lucy Jenkins heartily congratulated Alba for her extraordinary performance.

Alba threw off her bed covers and put on her dressing gown and slippers. On impulse, she crept quietly downstairs and opened the back door. The full moon shone brightly, illuminating the whole garden. The night sky was very clear. The myriad stars were so visible that Alba drew in her breath. She felt the stars were all around her in their beauty. The stone seat looked even more mysterious now in the moonlight. Alba walked quietly towards it. She placed her hand gently on the cool stone and sat down. Her thoughts turned to the Lady of the Flowers.

Alba realised that she had not yet asked the lady to identify herself. Their conversations were so interesting and helpful that this had not occurred to her. Alba thought about this. She had begun to trust the lady's wise words and gentle manner. All the conversations were about teaching Alba to trust in herself and find her own truth. She decided to trust in her intuition and continue to have the conversations.

'Who are you really, I wonder?' whispered Alba softly. She closed her eyes, content just to sit quietly for a little longer beneath the starry sky.

'Perhaps, somewhere in the silence is the answer to this mystery,' she thought.